# Seeds of Laveau

by

**_Ralph M Edgerson Jr_**

ISBN 978-1-943159-28-4

The publisher would appreciate notification where errors occur so that they may be corrected in subsequent printing and/or editions. Please send comments to the publisher by emailing to deeprivers67@yahoo.com Printed in the United States of America

<u>**Dedication:**</u>

*This book is dedicated to my beautiful, caring, loving and number 1 fan, my wife Darlene D. Edgerson. To my inspirations, my beautiful children, The Gamer, Ralph III and The Artist, Bryanna Nykole. Because without them in my life, I would definitely not be me. And to the city that taught me so much, the ever so beautiful and forever home,*

*New Orleans, La.*

## *INTRO*

The tales of Marie Laveau stretch across numerous stories of Herbalist, Politician, Socialite, Psychic and most of all The Queen of Voodoo. Her offspring had to be destined for greatness or so we think. The continuous battle between good and evil had to be present in order for this powerful being to come forth. So, the same battle must continue for her seeds. The city of New Orleans is only the backdrop to this tale of beings embracing their fortune or misfortune, depending on how one would see it. The year was 1994, the city was fighting with itself as violent crime was on the rise, murders were occurring every day and city officials didn't know what to do to calm it all. A glimpse from the city's old history raised its head but at what cost. A seed only grows when it is watered with purpose.

### *What are Loa?*

Loa (pronounced loo-WAH[1]), are spirits in the West African and Haitian Voodoo religion. They have also been incorporated into some revivalist forms of Louisiana Voodoo. Many of the loa derive their identities in part from deities venerated in the traditional religions of West Africa. In Haitian Voodoo, the loa serve as intermediaries between humanity and Bondye, a transcendent creator divinity. Voodooists believe that over a thousand loa exist, the names of at least 232 of which are recorded. Each loa has its own personality and is associated with specific colors and objects. They expect to be properly served, not just communicated with. They are each distinct beings with their own personal likes and dislikes, distinct sacred rhythms, songs, dances, ritual symbols and special modes of service. The exact number of Loa are unknown and always changing, if you were to ask a voodoo practitioner, they would always add a plus one at the end. Many of them are equated with specific Roman Catholic Saints on the basis of similar characteristics or shared symbols.

## Chapter

Dèsirèe flopped all over her bed in her sleep as an occurring dream plagued her unconscious mind with images of a woman she had never seen before. No matter how the dream started or what it was, the mysterious woman always showed up with the same statement,

"Dark and Light surrounds the earth, but you reside in the grey. It's time you choose. Pick a side. PICK A SIDE!"

The dream would always scare Dèsirèe awake after the woman would shout at her but once awake, she would always feel as if someone was watching her. Dèsirèe Glapion was a college student in her last year of medical school and ready for her first year of residency at Children's Hospital of New Orleans. At a young age she suffered with nightmares but gained control of them as she got older. This nightmare felt so real to her, as if she was in it in real life and not in a dream state. Dèsirèe would at times feel as if someone would be holding her wrist like in her dreams even after she was awake. The moments scared her, but she would shake them off and get back to her normal day-to-day.

Dèsirèe lived with her grandfather Robert-Earl Glapion, an old soul who knew all the ends and outs of the history of New Orleans. Bobby, as family and friends would call him, always kept a real good story tucked in his denim overalls for anyone that was interested in listening to him. The two lived together for a few reasons but mainly to comfort one another. Dèsirèe's parents died in a car accident when she was just 11 years old and Bobby's wife, Dèsirèe's grandmother passed away a year later. The two have been inseparable ever since. Robert-Earl gave his granddaughter her privacy, not wanting to be a bother to the 21-year-old but he started noticing a change in his "Dizzy Bug". Dizzy Bug was a nickname he gave her years ago when Dèsirèe was just a toddler. Even though Bobby was pushing 77, he was very attentive to detail and could tell when something was out of place. He poured his granddaughter a cup of tea to get her morning started,

"Dizzy, you ok? You sleep good last night?"

"Not really Pop, a crazy dream kept waking me up."

"You know ya dreams is just yo conscious telling you what you needs to do, that's all Bug."

"Pop, I been having this dream for years nah. This old yella woman need to tell me then."

"Yella woman, wha cha mean chè?"

Dèsirèe started telling her grandfather about the reoccurring dream she's been having, and Robert-Earl sat back to take it all in. The sleepy and drained granddaughter wasn't ready for her grandfather's response though. Bobby started off by asking Dèsirèe if she knew of her family's history and not just the sweet memories of her childhood. She was a little vague on the subject because other than the fairytales she heard from her grandparents; she didn't know much. Dèsirèe wasn't in the mood for the old folk tales her loving grandfather would always be ready to share. But her attention brought her to the edge of the chair when he described the woman in her dreams without giving him one detail of her. The name Marie Laveau slipped from Robert-Earl's lips and a chill came over Dèsirèe like a wave.


Robert-Earl's description of the light-skin toned middle-aged woman dressed in 19th-century clothing was eerie to his granddaughter, but she couldn't turn away. He talked to her about an extremely powerful woman, power beyond what a person imagines power to be. Bobby explained to Dèsirèe her connection to her, and the young 21-year-old didn't know which way was up. Her mind rambled with questions, she doubted everything that escaped her aging grandfather's mouth,

"C'mon now Pop. You telling me I'm a descendent to a Voodoo Witch."

"She wasn't a witch."

"My bad, a Voodoo Queen."

"Chè, your bloodline is strong. So strong that you carry her strengths and with that strength a connection far beyond what you could understand right now."

"Pop, I gotta get to class for this exam I know I'm a probably fail, cause I ain't get no sleep, then I gotta go to work. I'm a see you later tonight, ok? Love you Pop."

"Love you too Bug."

Dèsirèe didn't know what to take of her granddad's story but his words continued to ring in her ear like a broken record. Everybody that ever lived in New Orleans knew of the fable tales of the Voodoo Queen named Marie Laveau. The actual practice of voodoo had fell off with the introduction of Christianity to the city centuries ago. Dèsirèe didn't really know how deep her bloodline went with the famous New Orleans icon but her curiosity was triggered. But she attempted to put her newfound discovery of her family's lineage in the back of her mind as she sat in the classroom. The final exam she was about to take was crucial to her getting into an elite residency Dèsirèe had been eyeing for a minute. The professor's assistant handed out the thick exam papers to everyone in the class and the professor started the large digital clock in the front of the classroom. The tension was so intense in the room, everyone's head was buried deep in the papers in front of them. Dèsirèe whispered to herself,

"You got this bitch."

"Yes, you do", was a reply she heard back that startled her.

Dèsirèe quickly looked over her shoulder for the voice, but only noticed heads down into the exam in front of them. She didn't know what to think of it. She questioned herself, was she hearing things, is her psyche playing tricks on her? She turned back to her papers as she looked down at the row of seats in front of her and saw her bestie, Sonya Paris. Dèsirèe and Sonya had known each other since freshman year and the bond has been strong like blood sisters, even though they weren't. Sonya was the firecracker of the two, always ready to enjoy life to the fullest, while Dèsirèe was the calm and composed one. They complimented each other because where one was lacking the other took control. Dèsirèe didn't have any other siblings so to have Sonya be part of her life was like a sister she never had. Right when she saw her friend's smile Dèsirèe knew that was the voice she heard whisper back to her.


The classroom emptied out as the last few students left out but Dèsirèe and Sonya were the last couple of students remaining. Right when Dèsirèe wrote down her last answer to her last question the professor called time on the exam.

She nervously walked up and handed her teacher the finished exam and her bestie was right behind her doing the same. Dèsirèe walked out of the classroom confident that she did her best but at the same time skeptical. Sonya on the other hand was gloating that she succeeded at the test,

"Girl that was a hard one, but I know I aced that."

"You sure? Some of them questions was tricky. I had to reread shit just to make sure I was answering them right."

"Girl, we got this! Dr. Glapion and Dr. Paris coming to a hospital near you bih!"

"The first black doctors in both our families."

"Yes bitch!"

The girls laughed as they rushed off campus to head to work. They both worked at a hardware store on N Rampart Street right across from Louis Armstrong Park. The girls did more socializing than actual work because the store was right on the outskirts of the French Quarters and tourists right along with residents frequent the store front. As always Sonya was the outgoing one of the two and men were drawn into her hazel-green eyes. The light brown beach sand skin tone complimented her eyes and was like a hypnotic attraction for anyone that spoke with her. Sonya used it to her advantage on several occasions when getting customers to buy unnecessary items from the store. Dèsirèe had to use her ingenuity but she got the job done as well and the two fought for employee of the month on a few occasions. During a break when they didn't have many customers, Dèsirèe told her friend about the conversation she had with her grandfather. When she told Sonya about the night visions she had been having, she was shocked that her friend had been having similar dreams. Sonya right along with her younger sister Trinity have been plagued with nightmares of the light skin woman since they were young,

"Girl, I always figured it was from something we looked at on TV when we were kids. Some horror show that fucked with us bad."

"The lady ever talk to you?"

"Nah, most of the time all she would do is point to a dark ass forest and show me some horrible shit. She be talkin' to you? I don't think I could take it. Dem damn dreams be scary as shit sometimes."

The terrifying illusions drew the girls closer to each other as they described what went on in them and Dèsirèe wanted answers. The sky darkened with grey storm clouds and the heavens opened up to a downpour. The rain slowed business down to a halt and the girls took that opportunity to ask to leave early for the day, they both had plans for research on their minds. Dèsirèe drove to the public library on Loyola Avenue and the two went in search for anything that involved information on Marie Laveau. This was 1994 and the internet was just getting its jump start. So, searching for archives like Laveau's history or in her case HERstory laid deep between the pages of some old books. It turned into an investigation, like they were two detectives looking for answers to a cold case. They both had an armful of biographies on the Queen of Voodoo and books after books on the history of New Orleans that included her in them. The girls were entrenched in reading when a set of twins by the names of Lucas and Eli walked up to their table. Sonya didn't even look up as she addressed them,

"Can I help you?"

"My apologies but my brother and I was wondering if you were finished with this book here."

"Which one?"

"The one named Voodoo in New Orleans."

"I guess. What are you looking for in it?"

When Lucas mentioned the name of the Voodoo Queen and why he and his brother was researching her, Dèsirèe asked them to sit with them. Eli and Lucas Trudeau eagerly sat with the ladies to continue their studies as they shared information with each other. The twins were the last of the very wealthy Trudeau lineage. A family that laid some of the groundwork for the city of New Orleans and made a lot of money from those endeavors. The twins didn't share most of the views of their well-off family members, like not associating with what they considered "commoners". Lucas and Eli felt more at home with people that didn't have as much as they did because they were more genuine rather than stuck up. The twins noticed something in the girls at the table besides the newfound interest in the mysterious woman in their dreams. The four created a bond and the search was on for the reason of the elaborate nightmares they all were having. Dèsirèe was amazed that her last name along with Sonya's last name was connected to the Laveau line. With Glapion being the last name of Marie Laveau's last husband and Paris being the last name of the Queen's first husband who introduced her to the voodoo practice. The coincidence was too intriguing for the group, and it got even more suspenseful when the twins noticed that one of their friend's last names were mentioned. Douglas Santiago was a childhood friend of the boys, and they couldn't wait to get in touch with him on the subject.

Lucas called his friend Douglas at home and was astounded that he knew all about the history of Marie Laveau. The girls listened as the two young men had a brief conversation on the phone about the subject in front of the library. Dèsirèe wanted to know more and asked if Douglas didn't mind if they all meet up. Douglas was more than happy to have the company; it was a subject he delighted in because the morbid and dark side of voodoo captivated him. Douglas Santiago was 8 generations deep into the actual studies of the voodoo practice and kept the practice going from what his father's father taught him. To find a small group that was interested in what he was doing brought Douglas extreme joy and he was eager to share all his beliefs with them. But he knew to be careful, because most people weren't ready for the truths he had to bestow on them. He called his cousin Saivon to come over because she was very fluent in the practice herself. Saivon Cantrell was deeply enthralled in the practice of voodoo because of her family connection with Douglas and her father's Haitian background. She tried her best to mask herself to be just like the famed Queen but mostly it was just an amateur imitation of the icon. Douglas and Saivon prepped themselves for all the questions they would be surrounded with as the group made their way to them. Douglas told his cousin not to get too overzealous with the rookies,

"You know everybody won't accept the studies with open arms. Most of them just looking for a trinket to take home with them to say they know about laws."

"C'mon Dee, they may be the ones we were looking for. Lucas said the other two had strong connections to the line, a connection we been searching for."

Douglas was sketchy when it came to believers of the craft but just like his cousin, he was anxious to see the Paris and Glapion girls. He pulled out books after books that couldn't be found in any library or book collectors' storage. Old books that creak when opened, yellowish brown pages that announce when they are being turned, handwritten paragraphs in old English and French Creole. Douglas was pulling it all out for his upcoming visitors eager to share his studies.

The storm battered the city of New Orleans, with sheets of rain as the thunder roared and lightning clapped across the skyline. The crew of four pulled up in front of Douglas's house on Dumaine Street, a raised double-sided shotgun house sitting on large concrete cinderblocks. Douglas watched them park in front of his house and opened the front door for them as they rushed inside away from the rain. Dèsirèe allowed her eyes to focus as everyone shook the rain off at the door. Lucas introduced his new acquaintances,

"Hey Doug, thanks for having us over dude. This is Sonya and Dèsirèe, the two I told you about."

"Thank you for having us. I know this is a little sudden, but Lucas and Eli said you knew a lot about this lady we been researching."

"Sonya, right? She is not just any lady, but the true Queen of Voodoo, the giver and taker of it all. But we will get into all of that in a minute, welcome to my home and make yourselves comfortable."

Eli started telling the host why they all were there, and Douglas listened with ears of excitement because he felt it was a connection from the spirit world. The visitors could see the passion in Douglas's eyes as he explained that nothing like what they were experiencing had ever been recorded before. The fact that all four of them, including Sonya's sister, were having the same or similar dream of Marie Laveau meant a lot more than their imaginations. Douglas walked everyone to the back of the shotgun house and Sonya couldn't help but to notice all the voodoo-enriched items all over. Dèsirèe noticed all the items too but she was more concerned about being in a stranger's home for the first time. She could get along with anyone, if the feeling was right but the unknown just had Dèsirèe a little uneasy. She had a knack for feeling people out when she first meets them, and Douglas was just a little too weird for her taste. The weirdness climbed up another level when Douglas walked them through a beaded curtain that opened up to the last room of the house. Saivon was seated at a round wooden table in the middle of the room, holding a very large dark green snake that coiled itself around her forearm. The only light came from a few candles that were perched on wrought iron candleholders. The room carried a scent of burning incense and dried-out flowers as the crew slowly marched in. Douglas offered all of them a seat as he took a seat next to his cousin and Sonya just thought the whole scene was hilarious. She nudged her friend who was wide-eyed at all the paraphernalia in the room, but Sonya's gestures offended Douglas. He stood up to address the group,

"If you not gone take this serious, please leave my home. This is my faith; this is my crest and I take it very seriously."

"My bad, but this a lot to take in. I only seen shit like this on scary movies and documentaries about the cult."

"Trust me, this is no cult. Voodoo is a spiritual journey like no other, a faith, a religion and an awakening."

"I'm not trying to join a religion. I just wanna get some answers."

"Sister, you're already part of it. There's no need for you to join."

Dèsirèe and Sonya sat wondering what Douglas meant by his statement. The host along with his cousin started explaining to them all about the blood line of Marie Laveau and how they all were connected to her. Lucas and Eli carried the last name of Laveau's biological father Charles Trudeau. He was a very prominent figure in New Orleans, owning several properties throughout the French Quarters. Douglas explained that the Paris name was connected to the Santiago name, which was the Voodoo Queen's first husband's last names and that connected them to each other. From the books she scanned through at the library, Dèsirèe knew her last name was closely related to Laveau's last husband but didn't believe that made them blood relatives. She figured slavery in the south made her being related to Marie Laveau unlikely because a lot of newly freed slaves changed their names. Saivon assured Dèsirèe and the rest of the group that their names wasn't the only thing that coupled them to the Queen. Right then everybody in the room was reminded that they shared an even stranger bond and that was their night illusions. Douglas pulled a thick leather-bound book from a shelf, opened it and began sifting through the aged sheets. The storm outside announced it was still around when the sound of thunder rattled the old house and the continuous taps of raindrops slapped against the roof. Eli was trying to read the words in the book Douglas was holding when his eyes fell upon his last name and noticed mayor next to it,

"Trudeau was a mayor?"

"Acting mayor really, the previous one died and he stepped in."

"So Laveau's father had a little power."

"That political power trickled down to his daughter too."

Saivon started to tell them how the Queen's political power went hand and hand with her spiritual strengths. The group sat for a few hours learning about their heritage and what it could mean for them. Dèsirèe was still a little suspicious of the whole thing, but another side came out of Sonya. The Paris girl was trying to see how she could make everything work in her favor and never have to work again. Everybody took it as if she was joking but deep-down Sonya was serious. Lucas' belly began to rumble from hunger, and everyone started to realize they had been by Douglas's home for a long time. They all made their way out and the host made himself available to them anytime, telling them they could always come over to discuss the culture.


Dèsirèe was heading home with all sorts of things flowing through her head but the key thing that frightened her was what did the mystery woman in her dreams want. She noted the excitement on Sonya's face on the subject and wondered why she wasn't feeling the same. The young Glapion girl knew something was coming but didn't know what and couldn't wait to get home to talk to her grandfather. She knew one thing her loving papa would make her feel better about it all. Dèsirèe finally made it home to find her grandpa sitting on the porch puffing on one of his cigars. After the storm cleared, Robert-Earl enjoyed the smells in the air. A slight grin came over his face when he seen his grandbaby get out of her car,

"Got some crawfish etouffee and fried catfish on the stove if ya hungry."

"Thanks Pops. Can I ask you something?"

"Anything Bug. What's wrong?"

"Is Voodoo good or evil? I heard some call it a religion and others call it a cult. What is it?"

"Now that right there depends on who you talking to. Cause any religion has its faults. You talking bout human beings here."

Dèsirèe listened as her grandfather explained his explanation of the religion her bloodline is so closely related to. How it dates back thousands of years before Christianity and how it was adapted from Haiti along with being intertwined with the Catholic religion in New Orleans. Robert-Earl gave his grandchild way more than she expected when he elaborated how her distant relative used her strengths for good. How if it wasn't for her influence a lot of liberties slaves had in New Orleans wouldn't have been thought of. Dèsirèe viewed Marie Laveau in a new light and not the dark gloom that was cast on the hometown icon from rumors. Her status was in her name which heightened her status in certain classes of people. Robert-Earl told stories of Laveau attending closed chamber meetings with city officials on the subject of slaves and their treatment. How at a young age before she was crowned the Queen of Voodoo, Marie Laveau had a status of prominence in the city. All the high praise gave Dèsirèe a better view of the icon, but it still didn't answer the dreams she was having. The young woman had questions her grandfather for once couldn't answer for her.


       Sonya couldn't wait to tell her sister Trinity all about her experience at Douglas's house. She went on and on about how powerful Marie Laveau was and how the residents of the city feared or respected her. Trinity was on the same page as her sister's friend Dèsirèe, who wondered why she was having the disturbing dreams. All the extra stuff Sonya was talking about didn't concern her because at this point Trinity was concerned about what the Creole woman in her dreams wanted. Why were the nightmares happening to them and what was the connection to it all? Trinity Paris was a first-year college student, only 3 years younger than her older sister Sonya but wise beyond her years. She studied to be an Architect because at an early age Trinity was fascinated with building structures, especially New Orleans architecture. The intricate designs of combined modern and colonial intrigued her to one day be a part of the discussion of what she considered artist of the city. Trinity was done talking to her sister about her Voodoo experience and went to bed in hope of getting a good night's sleep. Sonya fiddled with her hair in her vanity mirror, with thoughts of becoming deeper in the Voodoo circle. She imagined dreams of being as powerful as the stories that were told to her about Marie Laveau.

As she daydreamed a shadow passing behind her caught Sonya's attention in the mirror and she quickly turned around to see no one. Figuring it was nothing, Sonya went to get ready for bed but then heard someone talking in a whisper,

"It can be yours. It can be all yours."

Thinking her sister was teasing with her she swung her bedroom door open to find no one there. Sonya thought the weed she smoked on her way home had her hallucinating as she closed her door and laughed it off but then a shadowed figure stood in front of her. She wanted to scream but her voice escaped her as the dark figure spoke to her in several different tongues. The thing that Sonya couldn't understand was that she understood every word the dark spirit said to her. It told her that she is the chosen one of the spirits and that she will reign over all those beneath her. Sonya listened as the shadow gave her instructions to collect servants that would lift her to power and familiar names came across her eyes. Douglas and Saivon were a part of the long list that the spirit gave her with images of heightened influence over the city of New Orleans. Sonya started to embrace the thoughts that were implanted in her,

"I want it all."

"You will have it. They will sacrifice to you. They will fall to your feet. Follow my words and it will be done."

The greed had come over Sonya at that moment and all she saw was her strength increasing as the dark figure laid its hand on her. The dream she had been having for so long came in full color to her as she stood in a dark forest, but she was the only light. Silhouettes of people standing there worshiping her as the Queen and images of her foes laid at her feet. The oldest of the Paris girls had been taken over with a craving for the power she admired and the laughter of the dark spirit rang out across the realm.

## Chapter

A couple of months went by since their first meeting at Douglas's house. Lucas and Dèsirèe became good friends at that time, always checking on each other. Lucas wasn't exactly Dèsirèe's type, she was more attracted to the football jocks or bad boys and Lucas was more of the clean-cut caliber. Her attraction to a certain style of guy didn't deter Lucas one bit, he felt they had an attachment far beyond what any guy could give her. Even though he was crazy about Dèsirèe the first time he met her, Lucas held his composure and stayed in his lane, remaining her friend. The two took time out of their days just studying the history of Marie Laveau, the religion of Voodoo overseas and the craft practiced in New Orleans. The platonic couple were intrigued at how old the religion itself was, dating back way before settlers came to America and before the introduction of Christianity. Just like her grandfather told her, Dèsirèe discovered that just like any other religion, in the wrong hands it could be deadly. She and Lucas read tales of mistreatment, revenge spells cast and horrific mutations from conjuring up evil. Dèsirèe realized then that the bearer of the laws of Voodoo had a lot of responsibility. Good and evil went hand and hand, but it was up to the bearer to decipher the proper course to take. Trinity had joined the two on occasion because her sister Sonya seemed to not be as concerned about what everything meant. Little did they all know, Sonya had her own plans in the workings.

Even though Dèsirèe and Sonya remained really close friends, the entire group of seven split off into two separate groups. Sonya listened to the instructions from the Dark Spirit as she gathered her clan together with the cousins Douglas and Saivon. The cousins were thrilled to be a part of what Sonya explained would be in a word, magnificent as she shared her encounter with the Dark Spirit. They never had a spiritual encounter of any kind so hearing that someone they knew experienced it drew them in. Douglas also shared his passionate practice that he hadn't mastered to seize another person's body with a spell he found. Saivon informed Sonya that the spell could help greatly with their reign,

"Possessing another's body would put us in control. We could literally take over whoever we want and have them do whatever we want. Law enforcement, politicians, government officials could all be under our control."

"Yes. Master it and get it done. Find you a test subject to practice on but I must be there to witness it."

The group of three had ventured down a rabbit hole of no return but Sonya was like a shark, and she smelled blood. It was no stopping her at this point, as she dove deep into the practice, studying the craft more every day. She started off with simple gestures that led people to do her willing, but it all grew when Sonya opened herself up to a much darker joy of pleasure. Her beauty was already captivating to most men and using that as a portal Sonya had men willing to put themselves in danger for her. With a simple collection of herbs, stones, personal property and a few chosen words Sonya convinced one guy to abandon his family to protect her at all costs. The incantation was simple, but it was only the beginning to Sonya's strengths. She dug more into the craft and found so much more as Douglas shared more unknown books on the abilities of Voodoo. Dèsirèe on the other hand was studying deeply on how to help or better the next person than taking like her friend. Trinity, Lucas, Eli and Trinity's boyfriend Micah Augustus all were on the same page with Dèsirèe. Micah never experienced any of the nightmares the others had but he supported their cause. He and Trinity were high school sweethearts who grew into much more as Micah became more enthralled into Trinity's mission. They all went in search for those in need, using Dèsirèe's and Trinity's acquired strengths to help. The two young women gained an understanding of the dreams they were having and realized they both had a gift. Trinity used her gift to enhance her strengths with the abilities of Herbalist. Plant life spoke to her in a way as if it was talking to her like two people would have a conversation with one another. She knew the right combination of herbs to heal, help and strengthen someone's health in a way to lengthen their lifespan. Trinity loved the gift she received and pushed to better everyone around her. Dèsirèe's ability to read a person became something that went far past what she imagined. It went from just a feeling to literally a table of contents of a person's attributes when Dèsirèe spoke to someone. She could see their intentions, good or bad, like an aura that surrounded them like a glow. Dèsirèe could also see their pasts along with glimpses of their future and sway their decisions with a word if she chose to. Her strengths increased the more she practiced but she was cautious, scared that she would become power-hungry. Trinity was always there to encourage her,

"Dee, you are helping so many. We are helping so many. Don't ever hold back what gifts you have."

"Trinity, it's not that. It's just…I can feel something else lurking in the background. Like it's waiting for me to slip. Like once I do, it's too late."

"I understand where you coming from, because Sonya don't seem like herself anymore and I see it's no pulling her away from it. As for you, I gotchu."

The two didn't know their hard work was going to be challenged soon and other individuals would get involved. Some for the good cause Dèsirèe and Trinity were doing but also for the powers Sonya was seeking.

During his studies, Eli came across a captivating gentleman in the French Quarters working as a vendor. Baaloo was a Voodoo Priest that taught the religion to anyone that was willing to accept it in their lives. Like any other religious man, he held his faith to a great standard and expected the same from anyone that sought the truth. Eli approached Baaloo with questions and the priest was more than happy to answer them,

"How do I know I'm doing the right thing?"

"The Spirit will acknowledge you. Just like if you're doing wrong, that Spirit will acknowledge too. There's a Light Spirit right along with a Dark Spirit but it's up to you which side you care to join."

"Was Queen Laveau part of the Dark Spirit or the Light?"

"Now son, that depends on who you ask. She had a lot of Light in her, but her enemies would say she was part of the Dark."

Baaloo was delighted that the young man was so interested in the religion and asked him his reason behind his questions. When Eli told him about his friends the priest wanted to meet all of them and invited them over to his Temple close to Congo Square. Eli knew where the place was and told Baaloo that he would definitely come over to discuss the religion more with him. Talking with the priest gave the new believer a better sense of what he was doing as a whole. Unlike the girls, Lucas and Eli's gift was discovering potions that could be beneficial for their female counterparts. Invoking a spiritual strength wasn't in them and both of the boys were comfortable with that, they knew their purpose. Eli couldn't wait to call his brother after talking with Baaloo,

"Get in touch with Dee. We all gotta talk with this guy, he the truth."

"You sure he not some fake prophet just looking for a profit. We ain't got no money to give him."

"Nah. I don't think he like that bruh, he fareal."

Baaloo would be the first credited person the group would have ever spoken with since they started their quest. Lucas was a little uneasy because he knew how conniving some people could be. A lot of so-called Voodoo experts were just out there for money and exploitation of the craft because of the history of the city. Trinket shops, tour guides and more blanketed the city of New Orleans simply because of the status Marie Laveau carried over a hundred years ago. Eli's brother knew of the economic value the religion carried and the type of people who made money off of it. Even with his strong convictions about the situation, Lucas got in touch with Dèsirèe and Trinity to tell them about the priest who wanted to meet all of them.


Sonya had a meeting of her own to conduct with her followers who felt they had finally mastered the art of possession. Douglas studied book after book on the subject, he felt he had the proper wording down and the correct ritual perfected in his head. Saivon was right there with him holding the same level of excitement for the upcoming event, they just needed a subject to test it on. As the two went over the practiced ritual Sonya's patience grew thin with them and her frustrations showed across her face. She was also working on a few tricks of her own and the constant clamor of the cousins kept breaking her concentration. Right when Sonya was about to shout Douglas heard a knock at the back door of his house. He wasn't expecting any visitors and attempted to ignore the knocks but the person on the other side of the door wanted in as they knocked harder. The sound echoed through the house as if someone was trying to beat the door down. The homeowner pulled a large kitchen knife from the counter in front of him and shouted,

"Unless you wanna meet your maker. You best get from by my door!"

"My maker sent me to your door. I speak from the lips of the Spirit. You may want to hear from me."

With the spell-tranced bodyguard, she still had control of standing at her side, Sonya told Douglas to open the door. She wanted to see who this person was because the voice carried meaning to her. Douglas slowly opened the backdoor to a man dressed in an all-black Seersucker suit, adorned with a bright red rose in the top pocket. He walked in, made himself at home, sat down in a chair in the corner, lit a pipe he got from his inside coat pocket and smiled at them all. The aged face of the man that just interrupted their meeting seemed familiar to Sonya. It was as if she had seen him before, but she couldn't put her finger on it,

"Can we help you?"

"The question is, what can I do to help you?"

"I'm really not in the mood for riddles. I allowed you in here. Please don't have me make you leave. Cause I can have ya walk for days, until ya feet bleed."

"I believe you can, but Spirit won't be pleased with your actions. See, Spirit sent me here because you Sonya, needed to find me. My name is Baka."

Right then Sonya realized where she knew the face. It was one of the faces Dark Spirit showed to her when it gave her the list she needed. Baka was a Voodoo Doctor who practiced heavily on the dark side of the faith. The side of Voodoo that was idolized for centuries, profited upon by the wicked and commercialized by the greedy. Baka was an experienced illusionist by craft and a faithful Hoodoo worshiper with the gift of gab. Some may say Voodoo and Hoodoo go hand and hand, but the slight differences can lead to life or death. Saivon's pet snake found its way draped over Baka's shoulders as he continued with his speech. The three listened as the Voodoo Doctor preached visions of power using tarot cards and animal bones. Everything that exited his lips seemed like a riddle, but Sonya understood she would have to terminate some friends if she was to gain the strengths she wanted. Douglas felt he knew enough about the craft that he nor his associates needed Baka and the Doctor found the young man amusing. Baka reached in his pocket, pulling out a small cloth bag and handed it to Douglas,

"My boy, you have only touched the surface of your power. Allow me to open you to so much more."

"I don't want your lunch old man."

"By the time I'm finished with you, you will feed on the weak."

With just a few words from Baka, the group expanded one more soul and Sonya felt her strengths increasing. The addition of the Voodoo Doctor also added an insight to the right government officials who believed in her powers. The greed grew in her and nothing or no one was going to stand in Sonya's way on her voyage to be the most powerful woman in New Orleans.

__________________________________________**3rd**

**<u>Chapter</u>**

The crew all met up at the Voodoo Spiritual Temple across from Congo Square. Dèsirèe read articles on rituals performed at East African Voodoo Temples and her expectations were far from what she walked in on. The New Orleans style of Voodoo practices weren't quite what she thought was going to happen. Baaloo seemed like an everyday priest standing at his altar going over tomorrow's sermon, searching through the Bible for the right verse to clarify his point. The Temple resembled a normal church that had Catholic innuendoes, Voodoo cultures and a bit of African flair. An assortment of African masks, Catholic statues, and Voodoo art canvased the walls. Baaloo looked up from his spiritual books to see the young group walk up the aisle of his Temple. An impressed smile came over the religious man,

"Brother Eli, you really came. I'm pleased."

"I said I would."

"And I see you convinced your friends I wasn't a prophet in search of a profit."

"We had our doubts."

"I don't blame you brothers and sisters. New Orleans has been plagued with those looking to enhance their pockets off what non-believers consider a magical mystery. By doing so they diluted the purity of the faith."

Eli looked over at his brother because it was pretty much the same words, he had just finished telling him over the phone. Lucas stood there corrected after hearing Baaloo explain his distaste for the religious leaders that continue to drain their congregation of money. The Voodoo Priest believed the Temple was his responsibility and sharing his word was his pleasure. If a member of his congregation had money to give, he would happily accept it but if they didn't have any to give Baaloo would be fine with that also. The young group completely agreed with Baaloo's logic, and a plethora of questions came at him from all directions. Dèsirèe sat back silent as Baaloo tried his best to be as informative as possible with the crew. She took in everything the priest shared with them but at the same time questioned the reason she was chosen for this task. Baaloo could see the questions running in Dèsirèe's eyes,

"I can see something is on your mind sister. I'm an open book. Allow me to answer whatever questions you have. Or are you still skeptical of me or the faith?"

"I'm not a skeptic. At this point I am a believer."

"So, is it me? You've been silent the entire time. A silent soul is a thinking spirit."

"No, it's not you. Your glow is covered in blue, red, pink and a splash orange. I'm sorry, I see colors around people when I meet them."

"You're seeing their aura sister. Their aura tells you who they are. It takes years for most to

master that craft, but I see you're far beyond a
novice."

"Trust me, I am definitely still a novice."

Baaloo started to explain to Dèsirèe what she
was seeing and how it could benefit her. The
newly acquired young believer listened as the
priest enlightened her on her gift but Dèsirèe
wanted to know why she was chosen. She feared
gaining such a power could lead to a temptation
that she could lose control of. Dèsirèe saw
people change into evil individuals after gaining
simple levels of authority at school and work.
She knew this was much greater and had serious
consequences if mistreated. The priest
recognized her concern, encouraging her that she
was chosen because of her heart and if she ever
needed guidance, he would be there for her.
Dèsirèe began to see that Baaloo was genuine
with his words and the entire crew opened up to
him. They shared their gifts, trades and abilities
with him and Baaloo shared his. The priest
shared his knowledge of the religion with them,
its background and a lot they didn't know about
the faith they found themselves in. They all
soaked in every word until late in the night. The
group didn't want to leave but everyone had to
get home and so did Baaloo, so they ended their
learning session for the day. Dèsirèe took Trinity
and Micah home while the Trudeau brothers
went the other way.

Lucas stopped at Triangle Deli to grab them a bite to eat when Eli noticed their friend Saivon walking across the street. The younger of the Trudeau twins called out for his old friend who seemed to be searching for something. Cars buzzed past the unconcerned Saivon as she casually walked across busy Broad Street. After catching his friend's attention Eli walked to the corner to wait for Saivon to meet him, but then he heard a whisper behind him. When Eli turned around, there stood Douglas who quickly blew a white powder in Eli's face. Blinded from the powder as he staggered back away from the street, Eli could hear Saivon chanting an unfamiliar language. He attempted to get back to the car as he shouted,

"What da fuck Doug!"

The blurriness began to clear in his eyes when Eli gripped the door handle of the car to find that Saivon and Douglas were gone. Confused by what just happened, Eli got in the car still rubbing his burning eyes. Right then Lucas walked out of the deli unknowing of what just took place. He seen his brother's confusion and asked what was wrong, but when Eli tried to tell him what happened Douglas showed up behind him with a whisper. Before Eli could say anything, Lucas turned around and experienced the same fate as his twin as Douglas blew the white powder in his face. As he tried to whip away the powdery substance that blinded him, Lucas could hear the chanting coming from

Saivon's lips. His vision cleared and no one was standing outside with him. Lucas rushed into the car locking the doors as he and his brother wondered what just happened. They wanted to get in touch with Dèsirèe, but fright kept them from getting to a phone. The abrupt sound of a car horn scared them when a deli customer blew trying to get them to move from in front of the store. Lucas pulled off heading home still confused to what just took place,

"What da fuck was that?"

"Dude just take me home."

"What da fuck!"

Lucas was seconds from their house, he and his brother were completely spooked about what just happened to them. Looking over their shoulders, staring down every car that passed them and repeatedly running every red light on the road. Eli didn't even allow the car to come to a complete stop before opening the passenger door so that he could get out. The twins thought they were finally safe when they stepped onto the porch of their home, but the two stalkers were right behind them. In their deliriousness the brothers failed to realize Douglas and Saivon were following them home. Douglas blew another whiff of his white powder in both of their faces and the twins fell to the floor in a panic. The cousins grabbed the brothers, dragging them through the front yard and shoving them in the backseat of their car. While

Lucas along with Eli laid there, blind to their surroundings, Saivon continued with her chant and the brothers felt as if their muscles stiffened. They were completely paralyzed, frozen in a sense as Saivon pulled a long dagger from her waist and Douglas held his hand over their faces. Saivon sliced into her cousin's hand with the dagger and the blood trickled from his palm, dripping in the twins faces. The hostages both could see what was happening but couldn't move one bit. Their minds strained so much to move one finger that they busted blood vessels in their eyes. Saivon started chanting again as she climbed in the backseat, straddling over Lucas and pushed the blade into his chest. He couldn't scream, he couldn't fight for his life and he ceased to exist as his body died. Eli watched as his brother died in front of him and Saivon just stared at the body. She looked at her cousin,

"When is he supposed to get up? I thought he was just gonna wake up."

"I don't know!"

"Should we just do the other one?"

"Do it before he start moving."

Eli was laying across the floor of the car and Saivon reached down, pulling him up to her by the hair. She placed the blade across his throat and began her chant for the ritual. Once the final words of the ritual was completed Saivon ran the blade of the dagger across Eli's skin slicing into his flesh releasing his blood down his chest. The terrified soul could feel his life fading as his shirt became soaked in his blood. His heart pounding, his mind racing but he couldn't do anything to stop the inevitable death. His eyes were focused on the passing streetlights through the front windshield of the car until the lights went from dim to dark. Eli knew he was gone but could still hear Saivon and Douglas going on about wasted souls. The words continued to echo in his ear over and over again until it sounded as if they were far away. The young Trudeau boy felt as if he was floating away, out of the car, through a nearby forest and into the darkness. Right when he began to see a bright white light Eli started to hear Douglas's voice again and his voice only became louder. The bright light he was heading towards started to move away, images of blood flashed in his head and Eli was being pulled back through the forest, right back into the car. His eyes opened, his lungs took in a gasp of air and a dead Eli was alive again, sitting up in the backseat of the car. He tried to speak but Saivon had sewn his lips shut with thick thread and the only sound that came out were moans. Eli turned to see his brother still laying there lifeless, eyes still fixed wide open but not one muscle moving. The images of blood and bones repeatedly sparked in his mind as he could hear the joyous shouts coming from the body snatchers in the car. Eli tried to resist him but when Douglas ordered him to sit up in the seat his muscles listened and did as it was told. Eli tried to fight but his body wouldn't move to his commands, only Douglas's voice could move him. Along with losing control of his muscles, he started to feel cold circulate through him, a cold like no other. The thump of his heart slowly beating became overbearing to hear and the wasted soul knew he was in trouble. The horrific images continued in Eli's head as Douglas cheered,

"We did it! We didn't possess him, but we made a fucking zombie! We made a fucking zombie!"

"You think Sonya gone be mad? She did wanna be here when we did it."

"Fuck that. Once she sees this, she ain't gone care bout not being here."

As Douglas drove down the dark road the only thing Eli could do was focus back on the passing streetlights through the front windshield of the car. Sounds of Saivon chanting an unfamiliar language again filled the inside of the car as Douglas commanded Eli to sleep and his vision began to fade into darkness. Their voices could still be heard but the darkness surrounded him to no end.


Dèsirèe and Trinity had no idea what just happened to their friends while they were heading home. Micah had Dèsirèe drop him off at The Detox House where he was an on-call counselor for recovering addicts. He and the Director of the Halfway House, Father Toussaint watched over a large number of drug abusers in search of recovery from their addiction. The Detox House was right on the outskirts of the lower 9th ward in Chalmette, a city outside of New Orleans city limits. The city held a reputation for being a little racist at times and some areas still practiced segregation even in 1994. Most of the residents of New Orleans didn't venture into Chalmette unless they had family members that lived there. After dropping Micah off at work, the duo began to head back to Dèsirèe's place but red, blue and white lights behind them caught their attention. A Chalmette Sheriff car came up fast and the loudspeaker instructed them to pull over to the side of the road. Trinity looked over to her friend as she made a joke,

"What you do? Yo ass got warrants?"

"Girl stop."

"I'm just saying, if we need to run let me know."

"Fareal, you play too much. What he want?"

They parked on the low-lit Judge Perez Dr alongside an old chain link fence that had overgrown weeds take it over. Dèsirèe waited with two hands on the steering wheel as the bright spotlight from the squad car lit up the inside of her car. The two were blinded for a second but then a terrifying sight stepped out of the law enforcement vehicle. Dèsirèe looked through her side mirrors to see a grotesque image of a slimy green lizard man in a sheriff's uniform. Hideous yellow eyes bulged from a green-scaled face with a forked tongue flickering from salivating lips. The monster slowly walked up to the side of Dèsirèe's vehicle as his clawed hands grazed alongside the door panel. Trinity had no idea what the driver was witnessing but could tell her friend was frozen in fear. Dèsirèe shivered as the officer came to the driver's side window but once he stood in front of her a human image stared back at her. The lizardman was gone and Officer Milson stood at the driver's side of the car tapping on the window for Dèsirèe to roll it down. Still frightened at what she witnessed in the mirror, the driver slowly let the window fall,

"Yes officer."

"License, insurance and registration."

"Here you go."

"Where you going gurl? You don't look like you from round here."

"Did I do something wrong?"

"I'm asking the questions here dammit."

"I'm sorry. We just dropped a friend off at work."

"You niggers know you don't work."

"Excuse me."

Right then, a flash of the lizardman stared at Dèsirèe with evil intent. Glows of green, purple and red surrounded him as he told the girls they don't belong in his town. They both were dumbfounded as the sheriff told them to get out of the car because he suspected drugs were in it. Hatred spewed from his lips as he gave disturbing descriptions of monkeys trying to take over as he shined a bright flashlight in the car's interior. Trinity's anger boiled inside as the racist continued his rant, yelling for them to place their hands on the hood of his vehicle. Dèsirèe, terrified of the horrific images flashing in front of her, immediately did what she was told. Trinity on the other hand was insubordinate and refused to place her hands on the hot hood. Officer Milson became enraged, whipping out his steel baton and stood in Trinity's face instructing her to put her hands on the police unit. Fearful of the consequences Dèsirèe cried for her friend to just do what she was told but Trinity was set in her ways. Sheriff Milson released a smirk right before striking the defiant young woman in the side of her thigh with the baton,

"You bout to learn some manners bitch! When I say move, you fucking move!"

"No! Please stop! She understands now."

"Shut up bitch. Before I come over there and give you some of this stick."

Trinity fell back, her legs in extreme pain, as she braced herself against the chain link fence. Officer Milson's attention was then directed towards Dèsirèe as he stood behind her and instructed her to spread her legs open. Trinity could hear whispers and thought the sheriff was giving out more demands. The racist officer then began frisking the detained suspect for any weapons or drugs. The degrading act was far from any professional search anyone ever performed in law enforcement. The whispers in Trinity's ear got louder and that's when she realized it wasn't from the people standing in front of her, but from the fence. The overgrown weeds on the fence were poison ivy and it offered to help Trinity,

"We are here for you. We are here for her."

Sheriff Milson groped Dèsirèe's breast, reaching under her shirt sliding his clammy hands on her skin and then pushed her head down to the hood of the car. The defenseless soul cried as the lizardman reached between her legs and caressed her genitalia with aggression. His aura was a gloomy green glow just like the reptile-scaled skin that covered his body and Dèsirèe no longer saw him as a human being, but a monster. Loud whispers came over her and the young woman began to chant to herself. At that moment Trinity began chanting also, still seated against the fence. Unknowing to the sexually aggressive lawman, the melodic chanting cause the weeds on the fence to reach out to him. Officer Milson shouted at the girls,

"Stop all that damn jiggaboo bullshit! You monkeys ain't in Africa."

Right then the vines of poison ivy quickly wrapped themselves around Milson's wrists and ankles, snatching him backward. The terrorist was now the terrified as he tried to shout for help, but a coil of vines pushed its way deep into his mouth. Trinity raised herself up from the ground and stared Officer Milson in his panicky eyes as Dèsirèe walked up beside her. Both women continued their chants as the vines squeezed tighter, pulling Milson flat against the fence. Trinity wanted to teach the racist a lesson he would never forget,

"You know those evil looks you were giving us when you seen two black girls in a car? You will never look at another person of color that way ever again."

Vines wrapped around the sheriff's head covering his eyes and began to rotate vigorously rubbing all the oils from the poison ivy leaves into his eyes. Muffled moans of pain came from his mouth as Dèsirèe had her own punishment to hand out to her assaulter. The angered young lady still had tears falling from her eyes as she whispered in his ear,

"You will walk until your children's children feet are tired. You won't stop until your ancestors apologize to my ancestors for what you did today. Now walk."

It was as if Officer Milson was in a trance, the vines released him from the fence and he walked away from them, heading west. The girls carried themselves back to Dèsirèe's car, secured themselves in the front seats and drove pass a marching Officer Milson whose eyes were swollen shut. They both had finally understood exactly how strong their powers truly were and it scared them.

4<sup>th</sup>

---

## Chapter

Two days had passed since the incident with Officer Milson and news reports of the missing Chalmette Sheriff Deputy stayed on every news station in New Orleans. Witnesses called in sightings of the missing deputy, but by the time law enforcement arrived there was no evidence of his presence. Dèsirèe feared what she and Trinity did would come out, but their concerns fell on the whereabouts of two individuals close to home. The missing deputy reports superseded two missing brothers with the media and the boys' family did all they could to find them. Flyers and personal search parties covered the city of New Orleans from Bullard Ave to Canal Blvd. Even Baaloo assisted with searching for the twins by passing out flyers at his Temple. Lucas's abandoned car in front of his house gave no clues to what happened to the Trudeau twins. Dèsirèe found it very suspicious how the twins just disappeared, and Trinity suspected the worst, especially after talking to her sister. The Paris girls started to pull away from each other spiritually and socially. Trinity felt that she was to be an aid to the community, but Sonya believed the world owed her. The separation grew larger when Trinity asked her big sister if she heard or knew where the twins could be. Sonya sarcastically replied,

"If they did what they was supposed to do, they would still be here. So as far as for them, so be it."

"How could you say that? They been nothing but nice to yo ass. Hell, they invited you into their home."

"Trinity, do I look like I care? Do I look like I give a fuck? Cause I don't. They got what they got, oh well. I'm trying to get this shit going for me and you can get out my way if you ain't gone help."

Sonya had bigger things on her mind other than worrying about two people that didn't mean shit to her, even though she knew their fate. The ambitious villainess figured she could start with getting some high-ranking people under her umbrella. Finding the missing deputy could put her in the good graces of the Chalmette Sheriff Department and strengthen her goal. So, Sonya reached out to the mayor of Chalmette, Mr. Sebastian Lacroix, and informed him that she was a psychic who may be able to help him. Through some snooping of her own, Sonya found out that the mayor was an admirer of the supernatural and used it to her benefit. She came to the conclusion that she could use her gift to convince him that she would find the deputy and in return, he would be indebted to her. Sonya's power of persuasion was easy on the mayor with a few words, and he was all in having her command the search for the missing deputy. There was no video footage of the incident, and the vacant squad car gave no clues to the deputy's location. Sonya had them bring her to the sight where they found Officer Milson's car and she was stunned at the images she received. Mental visuals of the missing deputy molesting someone Sonya knew personally and sparks of light as pure power surrounded them. The psychic medium could still feel Dèsirèe's power all around her and like breadcrumbs in a dense forest it sent a trail right up the road. Sonya put on a performance for the onlookers,

"He was standing right here, patrolling his streets but he was hit with confusion, stumbled over here by the fence and walked away. Your friend just walked away, heading that way. I can still see him going in this direction."

"Was anybody with him?"

"No. Cars passed him, but he is alone. He's in search of something."

She told them things that only the department knew that they didn't share with the media and pointed them to where they needed to look for the deputy. The tingling electricity buzzing all around Sonya had Dèsirèe's and Trinity's scent invading her senses. For the first time since she gained her new strengths, Sonya felt inferior and that brought on a rage inside her. With calculating intentions, she gave the deputies a fairytale explanation of where their comrade could be. Sonya didn't want anyone close to her newly found target who just happened to be a female she used to look at as a sister. Mayor Lacroix was too pleased with what his contracted medium came up with and offered to assist her whenever she needed him. The oblivious victim didn't know he had just invited the devil to his table and that invite opened up a conjuring spell that gave Sonya control of him. She left the mayor's office with the confidence that her plans were falling into place. Sonya stopped at a pay phone and called her obedient followers Douglas and Saivon to let them know she needed their zombie. She now had plans to eliminate what she felt was a pest and terminating a long friendship in the process. Sonya just needed to get her blood sister Trinity to go along with the scheme she had in mind.

Dèsirèe was at work helping a customer get supplies for a home project they were doing when she felt pressure push against her. It was as if someone stood in front of her and pushed her in the chest with the palms of their hands. Her body tingled as goosebumps crept up her arms and then Dèsirèe's attention pulled her to look towards the front door of the hardware shop. A shadowy figure engulfed the doorway as smokey black and green tentacles seeped through the cracks of the door seal. The door opened hitting the brass bell that hung right above it and like a trick from a magician Sonya emerged from the fog. Dèsirèe realized no one else could see what she just witnessed, and, in some way, Sonya knew that also when she released a smirk toward her fellow employee. The two didn't say a word to each other as Sonya went to the back of the store to get her apron. The antagonist grinned with evil intent as the shop filled with a static tension of the two opposites' protruding energies. It was as if they could see storm clouds fighting for position overhead while they were so close to one another. Dèsirèe finally knew something wasn't right with her close friend and waiting to find out more could be dangerous. Sonya's aura was covered in a glow of black and green with a ghostly figure standing at her side. Dèsirèe held her composure pretending that she was unbothered but inside she was petrified of what would happen next. Sonya's devilish grin became a nuisance to Dèsirèe as she watched her walk up to their manager and whisper in her ear. The manager in return spoke aloud to all the customers in the store,

"Excuse me everyone! Can you please leave the store? I must close up now there's been an emergency. I apologize for the inconvenience, but you must leave now."

The hardware store only had a handful of people in there and filing them out was easy as the manager escorted them all to the sidewalk. Dèsirèe had confusion written all over her face when she heard the front door lock engage and a glazed-eyed manager walked past her. Sonya laughed as she walked down the aisles of the shop towards Dèsirèe and the evil aura around her reached out knocking items off the shelves. Dèsirèe backed herself up as Sonya started her spill,

"I must admit, I would have never thought it would have been you, Dee. What you did to that cop was glorious. He deserved that shit, and I should have sent them people straight to your door. But you would have wormed yo way right out of they grasp. When did you know? Who came to you and showed you ya gift?"

"Sonya don't do this."

"Do what? Become the most powerful woman in NOLA? Yeah, I'm most definitely doing that shit."

"Sonya please I don't wanna do this."

"Too late, we doing this."

The Dark Spirit surrounded Dèsirèe pinning her against the wall as shadowed tentacles wrapped around her neck stopping her from breathing. Sonya's victim struggled to grab hold of smoky appendages that seemed to slip through her fingers. Dèsirèe fought until she couldn't fight anymore as she fell to the floor. Her body went limp, the Dark Spirit hovered over her ready to take in her soul and Sonya gloated with victory in her sights. The demise of her rival would boost her to the front because she knew everyone else would fall in line. Sonya watched as Dèsirèe tried to gasp for air and knew her last gasp was coming. The moment was coming but then a thick green vine wrapped around Dèsirèe's ankles and snatched her through to the back of the store. Sonya was infuriated and her rage lashed out in the form of everything being cleared off the shelves onto the floor. She rushed towards the back storage room where the vine pulled Dèsirèe to find Trinity standing guard over her friend,

"Sonya stop!"

"Trinity move!"

The smoked tentacles grabbed Trinity by the throat, lifting her off the floor and holding her out of Sonya's way. Right when she was able to focus on her victim taking air in her lungs a light radiated so bright from Dèsirèe it staggered Sonya back. Trinity fell to the floor and both of Sonya's casualties ran to the back exit. Dèsirèe pushed the exit door open so that they could escape from their assaulter only to run right into Eli and a mysterious man standing in the alleyway. The mystery man stood there smiling at them, but Eli's appearance was disturbing to see. His lips still sewn shut, his eyes whitened over, a deep slash across his neck, his skin looked clammy and a stench of dying flesh emitted from his body. Before the girls could react to Eli standing there, he grabbed Dèsirèe, shoved her in the back of Douglas's car and the vehicle sped off.

## <u>Chapter</u>

Trinity went into hiding after the attack on her and Dèsirèe at the hardware store. Police along with reporters classified the ransacked store on Rampart Street as vandalism and the investigation was closed. NOPD had more on their plate with rising murders everyday so a store being damaged by what they felt was rambunctious teens wasn't on their radar. Sonya tried using her powers to find her little sister, but Trinity managed to mask her energy from the villain. Two hours away from the city life in New Orleans, Dèsirèe was being dragged through dense swamp land in Breaux Bridge, Louisiana. Sliding through the mud, branches, occasional deep puddles and pulled by her feet, the victim was defenseless. Douglas and Saivon with the help of Baka stuffed a tied-up Dèsirèe in a pine box with her deceased friend Lucas who already had maggots ravishing his body. While the three lowered the wooden box into a muddy hole in the middle of the swamp, Eli helplessly watched. He couldn't move without Douglas giving him the command to, so he stood there silent. The feeling was worse than being undead, watching two people he cared about cast away like trash. After the makeshift grave was covered, Baka laid out a few artifacts on top of the mound,

"This will keep her here until our Queen is ready to deal with her."

"Our Queen? Sonya not my Queen."

"Girl! Don't let me hear you say that again. She will be the Voodoo Queen of all Louisiana real soon, just watch."

The three left the swamp, making their way back to New Orleans pleased with the deed they had just finished. Just like Sonya they felt they got rid of the one person that could stop them from taking over. Douglas unknowingly forgot to tell Eli to come with them and left him there standing in the swamp next to the grave. The undead soul stood there like a watchdog over the fresh grave while snakes, alligators and all sorts of swamp creatures roamed past him. It wasn't until Douglas was far away from Eli the spell that controlled him weakened and the poor soul was able to move on his own. He didn't want to leave Dèsirèe, but the artifacts Baka left behind were too strong for Eli to move away so that he could dig her out. The freed zombie went in search of someone that could.

Trinity listened to the land and followed where it told her to go in order to get away from her sister's rage. The one place Sonya's strengths couldn't reach was in the middle of nowhere and that was exactly where the refugee was headed. Trinity traveled for days hitchhiking and on foot to get as far away from her sister as possible until she found an abandoned fishing shack on the banks of the Atchafalaya River. The spot was secluded from all human beings, miles from the nearest small city and surrounded by large bald cypress trees. She didn't have food or water in the swamps, but the plant life all around her provided, to keep her safe and fed. When she was hungry, vegetation in the river trapped fish in its vines and pushed it to the shoreline. When she was thirsty large leaves collected puddles of water for her to drink and when she was cold it covered her like a blanket. Trinity didn't know or understand her full strength, but she knew she was protected for the time being. She studied her craft, honed her skills and prepared herself for the unavoidable, when Sonya would come knocking at her door. Trinity would spend hours meditating trying to empower herself to gain the courage to just go and face her sister but the love she still held for her restrained her steps. She was fighting between what she felt was right and how her heart cared for her sibling. It wasn't until she heard whispers coming from the trees that she discovered Sonya's true nature. Trinity listened as the leaves spoke of a traveler in the swamps,

"Find him and he will show you. Find him and help him go on."

Trinity didn't know who they were speaking of but when she noticed a man across the river walking along its banks, she knew it had to be him. She shouted out for him, but he continued to aimlessly truck forward until he recognized her standing on the shoreline waving him down. The traveler stopped and stared Trinity down for what felt like a minute, still like a statue and then he did the unthinkable. Trinity watched as the traveler began to walk toward her but there was a half-mile-wide rolling river between them. She literally thought the man committed suicide as his head disappeared under the flowing brown waters. Her eyes scanning the river looking for any sign of the man popping up for air, but nothing was there but water. The only life source she saw was a large alligator swimming against the current of the river as its tail swayed in the waters. Trinity backed away from the river assuming the worse and then the man emerged from the deeps walking towards her out of the river onto the shore. His resemblance was of a friend Trinity loss over a week ago but the image of him was horrific,

"No, no, no, no. What have they done to you?"

There standing in front of her was Eli, tattered clothing, sunken eyes, bruised greyish skin and open wounds all over his body. Trinity was terrified but emotional all the same as she looked over the works of a mad person. During her studies she read documents of people creating zombies and the devilish descriptions they gave but never viewed one in the flesh. The soulless, the undead, the condemned and it all screamed to her in visions. The flashes of bone, blood and innards filled Trinity's thoughts as she could see what haunts Eli's decaying mind. She attempted to cast it away, but they were connected mentally somehow, and it vexed her thoughts. Trinity knew of three people that were capable of doing such a dastardly act and only feared what the outcome of Eli's twin could have been. She walked him in her hide away to get him out of the elements and finally realized at that moment that her sister must be stopped.

After being buried alive and left for dead, Dèsirèe fell into a panic state as she fought to get herself loose from the rope that bound her wrists together. She was surrounded by complete darkness and the foul smell of decay ravaged her nasal passage. Moisture began to soak the wooden box and the repeated sounds of water dripping in started to allow hysteria to set in her mind. Dèsirèe didn't know if she was going to suffocate to death or drown in a sealed box and neither, was something she desired. She finally was able to get out of the restraints and immediately started to push on the lid of the coffin. The presence of Lucas's motionless body lying next to her was beyond dreadful, but it got worse when she started to hear his voice,

"Dee I wish I could help you, I really do."

Knowing she was sealed in a box with a dead man had Dèsirèe believing she was losing her mind, but she heard his voice again. It was as if Lucas was talking to her, and the trapped feminine flower refused to talk back. She was determined that her last breath was going to be wasted on getting out of the grave she was put in. Lucas continued to be Dèsirèe's unwanted company in the grave but then she heard two more voices calling out her name. The panicked victim truly thought she was losing her mind as the two women began telling her she needed to get out of the tomb she was in. Dèsirèe pushed and pushed until she couldn't anymore as she screamed in agony. The two women along with Lucas told her to calm down, turn around and push once again. She didn't want to listen to them, thinking she was going mad, but what they were saying made some sense. Dèsirèe turned around, got on her knees, put her back against the top of the box and pushed as if she was trying to stand. The wooden lid began to crack under pressure and dirt started to fall in the coffin. Filled with excitement, Dèsirèe continued to push her way up until the top broke open and she climbed her way through the mud. Wet soil covered her eyelids, nose and mouth as she sifted through to the top until she was able to breathe in fresh air. Dèsirèe was free from her entrapment in the middle of nowhere but three people stood there with smiles on their faces. One person she recognized as she called out his name,

"Lucas! How the hell? Am I dreaming? You're dead!"

"Unfortunately my love, yes I am. You did it! I knew you would."

"How is this possible? Am I dead? Who are they?"

"Hello Dèsirèe, I'm Felicite Paris and this is my sister Angelie. We understand that this may be disturbing and even frightening but it will all make sense soon my love."

The world began to spin, breathing became rapid and vertigo set in as the newly freed soul tried to focus on what was going on. The experience was too much for Dèsirèe as her body just collapsed to the muddy swamp floor and she passed out. She could still hear whispers and talking as she lay there thinking she had truly lost her mind. Dèsirèe then sat up and looked up at the three souls still standing in front of her. Lucas was dressed in the same clothes he had on in the pine box, but Felicite and Angelie both were dressed in clothing from the 1800's. The images were unnerving but Dèsirèe calmed herself with a quick meditation because she just survived being buried alive. She equated what she was seeing for that reason, but she still had questions and who better to ask,

"Lucas, what's going on? How are you here? I seen you in the box, you was…"

"I know my love, I know. We can answer everything for you but to answer your first question, there's a war going on."

"A war? Da hell."

"We need to move. You don't need to be here, if and when they come back."

Dèsirèe rose to her feet and went along with the plan because she knew she had very little fight in her if someone would show up. They all tracked through the swamps and Lucas began to explain why she was able to see three spirits that no longer dwelled in the living realm. Felicite and Angelie also revealed who they were to her. That they were Marie Laveau's daughters from her first marriage to Jacques Santiago Paris. Laveau's first husband was a Haitian refugee and the one that introduced the practice of Voodoo to her. Dèsirèe listened as they told her that she was special, that she held a power in her that allowed her to see far beyond a normal person. She knew her ability to see a person's aura and that tingling feeling she gets when someone is close to her was a tall tale sign of their personality, but Felicite told her it was so much more than that. Angelie expressed the importance of Dèsirèe's gift and how it could be a benefit if used right or a curse if used wrongly,

"My love, it behooves you that you meditate, practice and understand your gift. With it, you can conquer any enemy but use it against the weak and you might as well go back to that wooden box and seal yourself away forever."

"Well, I definitely don't want that."

"Well, it's time to get to work. As you can see, Sonya is far more advanced than you and she had a lot of help along the way to get her there."

Dèsirèe followed the spirits through the swamp as they led her away from danger. She learned a lot, asking questions when necessary and meditating on the answers. Reaching out to the ones left behind was a desire deep in her but Dèsirèe knew it could be detrimental to them all if she was found. So, she traveled deep through the marsh towards the Gulf of Mexico and found herself standing near the shipping docks in Plaquemine Parish. Dèsirèe knew she had to get as far away from Sonya's reach as possible and traveling across massive waters was the best route. She snuck pass dock workers, dipping behind crates and shipping containers until she came across a large ship getting ready to take off in the Gulf. Dèsirèe ran up the ramp and hid between two large shipping containers on the vessel. Her counterparts were right there with her but hiding her from the world was not part of their strengths. Dèsirèe found that out when a deckhand walked up on her. The man was yelling at her in a foreign language and the stowaway begged for him to be quiet. The ship's worker glowed with a bright pink aura all around him and Dèsirèe knew he was a compassionate man. She got on her knees, put her hands together as if she was praying and her eyes begged him to help her because she knew he couldn't understand her language. The gesture was acknowledged with the man reaching out his hand and helping Dèsirèe to her feet. He could see she had been through a lot and her clothing told him she hadn't washed in days, let alone eaten. The deckhand walked her to a room at the far end of the ship where there was a large collection of bright pink and red glowing souls just sitting. She stood at the door a little nervous as she watched the helper walk over to another man, who looked as if he carried authority on his shoulders and watched them whisper to each other. The man looked over the helper's shoulder at the stowaway standing in the doorway. Dèsirèe thought she was about to get thrown off the side of the ship into the sea as the man began walking toward her. Her heart was pounding so hard in her chest, she could hear it. The man reached out his right hand as a greeting,

"Welcome to Marie. You ever been to Vietnam? Cause this here is a nonstop voyage."


Once back in New Orleans, Douglas realized he had left his undead slave back in the middle of the swamps and disregarded it as if it was trash. He and Saivon were on a quest to create another reanimated being but needed a subject to use. The city had amble prospects to choose from because a rash of violent crimes were on the rise and the city morgue was filling up with bodies. Saivon used her savvy and gothic sex appeal on a mortician who was willing to let her in the morgue to see the bodies. The guy was into morbid acts and the goth girl smiling in his face looked the part. While the mortician was occupied with feeling all over Saivon's breast and ass, Douglas crept pass to find his next involuntary servant. The now zombie expert knew the heart and brain had to be intact for his conjuring to work so he searched for the right deceased subject. While his cousin had the morgue employee pleasing his sexual fetishes on her, Douglas found three drowning victims. The annoying sounds of X-rated sexual acts going on in the room right next to the storage freezer where he was, distracted Douglas for a moment, but he was determined. He laid the three individuals on the floor, two men along with a woman and began summoning the spell that would awaken them from their eternal sleep. The chanting Douglas was performing began to get loud and caught the mortician's attention,

"What the fuck is that?"

"None of your concern."

"Fuck you mean?"

Right when the morgue's employee tried to go see what the noise was, Saivon blew a sleeping dust in his face knocking the victim out cold.

After whispering a forgetful spell in his ear, Saivon ran to go see her cousin's work. Like a puppeteer with no strings, Douglas began moving the corpses with his words and with glazed over white eyes they listened. The two body thieves headed towards the exit and their undead slaves followed them right out the door with no question. Douglas was pleased with what he accomplished and was eager to do it again,

"We need to find another morgue. I could create an unstoppable army in one night."

"As long as I ain't gotta deal with another pervert, I'm good. Muthafucka wanted to toss my damn salad the whole time."

"Da fuck!"

"Not that I'm against it but can I get some dick please?"

"You fucking freak you! Let's go."

"What?"

Saivon found a mortuary right off of Prytania Street, Touro Infirmary and the two walked right in like they owned the place. The sweet soft speaking damsel in distress distracted the guard while Douglas went straight to where all the dead were stored. He found five candidates to enchant and like a magician walked out the side exit door with five additions to his dead army. They charted out their next spot to hit and headed straight there. The cousins became so good at collecting bodies that night that they had to steal a U-Haul truck just to transport them. The sun began to rise, and Douglas started searching for a spot to hide a moving truck holding 30 undead souls in the back. He knew he couldn't just park it on the street because his load would be discovered, and their work would crumble. Saivon suggested an abandoned warehouse right down the street from the Calio Projects. Douglas backed the truck in the warehouse and they both were confident that their cargo would be safe there. They figured if someone around was to go snooping, once they see 30 dead standing staring forward it would scare them off. Douglas was so ready to tell Sonya what he had set up, but Saivon wanted them to stay in control. She knew if Sonya got a hold of their zombies, she would use them for her own gains.

## Chapter

Ever since his high school sweetheart and Dèsirèe seemed to just disappear, Micah had been roughing it on his own. He had Baaloo along with Father Toussaint to confide in, but it wasn't his peers and Sonya wasn't someone he felt he could trust. With the twins still missing and not really knowing Douglas or Saivon, Micah stayed to himself most of the time. Baaloo had been telling him a lot of valuable truths but one of the most important ones was not to fall for tricks of the Devil. The Voodoo Priest was referring to enemies that disguise themselves as friends and after a brief conversation with Sonya, Micah had a feeling she wasn't the friendly type. The Voodoo connoisseur was more concerned with what Micah could do for her than finding his love even though that same person was her only sister. The desperate boyfriend resulted to searching for Trinity on his own until Baka told Sonya it would be in her best interest to find her sister,

"Queen, you don't need any loose ends just rummaging around."

"My sister is not a loose end."

"I understand she is your blood, but you don't want your blood to be your demise. Maybe you can talk her into working with you and not against you."

"You and Douglas go find her. And bring her back to me, unharmed. Me and Saivon got a few men we need under our thumb."

"Yes Queen."

With her words ringing in his ear Baka followed the one person he felt would lead him to Trinity and that was Micah. Sonya wasn't the only one the Dark Spirit granted gifts to in order to take over the city in search of eminent power. The Voodoo Doctor had a few tricks up his sleeve that his group didn't know and one of them was the art of shapeshifting along with sensing a person's energy. Baka could replicate any human being he wishes to if he sees them once, assuming their identity. It was a strength he acquired at a very young age when he first started to follow the dark side of the practice. He shadowed Micah because he knew the lovesick boyfriend's energy was connected to Trinity and that would lead a trail to her. The Voodoo Doctor just needed to be patient, but his counterpart's patience was running thin. Douglas was more hands-on and just wanted to beat the information out of Micah or turn him into one of his undead. The power-greedy zombie maker acquired a lust for the craft and itched for the chance to have Micah under his control,

"You over here looking for breadcrumbs and if you just let me turn him, we could have him sniff her out."

Baka loved the hunt and sitting back waiting for his prey to show a sign of weakness was the thrill he yearned for, so he ignored Douglas's request. The two followed Micah in Douglas's car to the Halfway House where he worked, and Douglas scoped out several candidates that could be his next victim. A rehab facility full of recovering addicts who could easily relapse was a perfect place for a person to vanish,

"No one would expect a thing if a few of these crackheads end up missing. I could have a horde of walkers."

"We not here for that. We need to find Trinity and he is gonna lead us right to her, he just don't know it yet."

Baka watched as Micah walked into the chapel of the halfway house and Father Toussaint greeted him at the door. He saw the perfect opportunity to get some much-needed information from the boyfriend and that's when he revealed one of his powers. The Voodoo Doctor shivered as his fingers clenched the dashboard of Douglas's car interior, he grunted like a bull as his skin bubbled and blistered. But like a snake shedding off old skin, the image of Baka that Douglas knew fell off and melted away into dust. The fresh skin that the passenger wore like a suit was oily and new, but it was all

Baka as he released his sinister smile. The exact image of the Catholic Priest that just welcomed Micah into the chapel sat right in the car with a baffled driver. Douglas sat there in complete shock with his eyes frozen open because he never witnessed such an act. The transformation frightened him but at the same time drew him in. Baka finalized his shapeshifting when he imitated Father Toussaint's voice and Douglas couldn't believe his eyes or ears,

"How the fuck you do that?"

"Spirit gives you what you need. You just have to be patient."

Baka told his partner to get rid of the priest while he goes after their original target. The two left the car and split up heading in opposite directions towards the halfway house. Douglas put on a performance as he went to the information desk looking distraught, pleading for the clerk to call Father Toussaint. He hadn't taken a bath in a few days, so the stench of rotten onions, soured armpits and dingy clothing spoke volumes. Just to get Douglas from in front of her the clerk quickly called for Father Toussaint and had the visitor wait in the hallway. While the actor waited for his mark to arrive, the impersonated priest waited for the real one to leave his chambers. Baka casually paced as people went about their day and he even went so far as to greet a few when they noticed him. Just as expected Father Toussaint rushed out of his office making his way to the front desk to speak with a desperate individual, at least that's what he thought. Baka crept through the office doors to find Micah sitting at Father Toussaint's desk,

"That was fast, I thought they said it was an emergency."

"Just another crackhead looking for a handout."

"Father!"

"My bad, poor soul looking for help."

"Father, you something else."

"So, what were we talking about?"

While Baka was in the office convincing Micah, he was the man he'd been trusting for years, Douglas had Father Toussaint believing he needed his help. The priest went into counselor mode as he tried to calm what he figured was a desperate addict looking for help. Douglas in return put on a show for the concerned man standing in front of him. They walked outside to the side of the building where there was a long sidewalk that ran alongside a partial wooden fence. Father Toussaint assured him that whatever he had done before coming to him was not his fault, that the drugs had taken over his mind. The destitute man seemed to be listening to the priest and Father Toussaint went in to put his arm over Douglas's shoulder. He was leaning against a short wooden fence with his head down and the counselor continued to whisper touching words to Douglas, but he didn't see the curved sharp dagger,

"What can I do to get you to come join me so I could truly help you."

"There is one thing. I need you to die!"

Douglas swung quickly before the priest could react and jammed the dagger into Father Toussaint's neck. The gargling sounds of blood filling the holy man's throat were like music to the assaulter as he watched Father Toussaint back away from him with wide terrified eyes. The body was in complete shock as the priest's hands couldn't grasp the handle of the dagger to get it out. His eyes stayed wide open, but his vision blurred as he stumbled about trying to get away from the man that just stabbed him. Douglas slowly stalked his prey as he watched the preacher stagger about, dripping pools of blood from the open wound. Father Toussaint finally fell face-first to the ground, his body giving up. Douglas turned him over and straddled the halfway house curator's chest. With a quick snatch, the dagger ripped through the victim's flesh exposing the inside of his neck and blood spattered everywhere. Douglas took a second to take pride in his work, then dug his finger in the wound and wrote a symbol on the dying priest's forehead. It was a symbol of dominance over the clergyman's body and Douglas quickly went into his chant as the life left the dead man's eyes. With only a few seconds to spare before someone sees them on the side of the building, Douglas reanimated Father Toussaint to be one of his undead. The bubbling sounds of blood pouring from the zombie's neck were just an addition to the moans it made as it waited for its orders. Hazed over white eyes stared out into nothingness as Douglas led the undead soul back to the chapel chambers where Baka and Micah were. Cautious not to have anyone see them Douglas snuck about with his servant close behind.


Not knowing exactly what his partner in crime had done, Baka was still in the image of Father Toussaint and casually talked with Micah. He finally got the young man to relax and open up about somethings the real Father Toussaint didn't know. Micah confessed that his girlfriend Trinity and her friends had been practicing voodoo. That a few of them, including Trinity, had acquired special abilities and he believed that gaining those powers was what caused them to disappear. The impersonating Father Toussaint listened as Micah spilled out his truths to him and his deepest concern to find Trinity. That's when Baka seen his opportunity to dig a little deeper into Micah's psyche,

"I truly want to help you son. Voodoo is not a practice you take lightly; it can be very dangerous in someone's hand that doesn't truly know how to use it. Has she said anything to you before that could lead you to her?"

"She always said if a person wanted to hide away from the world, Louisiana is the perfect place to do it if you had the right resources."

"Think son, you and Trinity have a strong connection like a bond of the hearts. You can feel her. Think hard. Her whereabouts is right inside you."

"She did say she always wanted to…"

Right when Micah was about to give Baka a clue to Trinity's hiding place Douglas rushed through Father Toussaint's office door. With the reanimated undead priest right behind Douglas, Micah didn't know what was going on and the still bleeding wound to the preacher's neck stated nothing but danger standing in the room. The innocent man rose to his feet with his head on a swivel ready to defend himself. Baka frustrated with his partner shouted at Douglas,

"You idiot! What were you thinking?"

"Father! What's going on!"

"Calm yourself son."

Baka placed his hand on Micah's shoulder, stared him in the eyes and sat him back down in the chair. The priest's replica leaned back against the edge of the office desk, folded his arms and like he revealed his supernatural gift to Douglas, Baka's skin peeled off from his body. Layer after layer of flesh fell to the floor, reducing into dust on the carpet. The wet new skin on Baka's face smiled at Micah with the evilest grin as the

pupils in his eyes were the last thing to change
on the villain's body. The revelation was
terrifying to the unknowing suspect and Micah
jumped out of his seat trying to get to the door.
The zombified Father Toussaint, with Douglas's
instructions, grabbed hold of Micah and held him
in a bearhug with his hand over the victim's
mouth. He struggled to get away, but the strength
of the living dead was too strong to escape, and
the grasp became tighter the more he moved.
Baka slowly walked up to the paranoid Micah
and made sure they made eye contact,

"I said calm yourself son."

Micah paced his breathing and settled himself
down but then Douglas blew a white dust in his
face making everything around him fade to black
as he fell asleep. The two culprits snuck through
the back exit of Father Toussaint's office
chambers, avoiding anyone seeing them walk out
with Micah and the undead priest. They got into
the car and made their way back to Douglas's
house as Baka had plans to get out all the
information he needed from his prisoner.


Saivon followed behind Sonya as they
made their way into the mayor's office because
the power-greedy vixen was in search of
expanding her reach in the city with a few
political figures. She already had Chalmette's
Mayor Lacroix under control after a private
erotic séance in his office. She casted a spell on

him and Mayor Lacroix was too busy fondling Sonya's full breast to realize that she was taking over his empire. The mayor's fetish for the macabre was the opening Sonya needed and she walked right in as she indulged in a little self-mutilation on the mayor's chest with a razor, carving symbols into his skin. She found pleasure in the blood thirsty act and the mayor found a dominating master to appease. Dark Spirit oozed from her lips as she spoke and engulfed them in their foreplay. Mayor Lacroix became part of Sonya's clan in that moment and his soul belonged to Dark Spirit. Thinking they were just enjoying an erotic blood lust act the mayor's ignorance blinded him. He didn't know the carvings in his chest was a binding spell that would have him do whatever Sonya wanted. After succeeding with one political figure, the villainess knew she needed more to complete her task. With Saivon's help she had an appointment with the New Orleans' mayor who had a secret thing for teenage girls. Sonya stepped to the secretary's desk with authority in her voice,

"Could you please let Mayor Morales know Sonya Paris is here to see him?"

"You have an appointment?"

"Of course I do love."

"Wait here and I'll get the mayor for you."

"Thank you baby. Oh, and that lil man of yours, if you keep letting him, he gone keep stepping

out on you. Make him some tea and he won't see
nobody but you."

The secretary was baffled that the young woman standing in front of her knew what she was going through at home. With the gifts Dark Spirit placed in her, Sonya could see the woman's struggles and gave her a gris-gris Saivon made. The oracle told the woman to believe in her strengths, make her spouse a cup of tea with the potion in her hand and all her worries would disappear. The secretary was skeptical of Sonya's words but when the visitor had her bodyguard come up and express his love for only her the executive assistant knew she was real. The mayor's 12 o'clock appointment waited patiently for the public figure to come greet them while the secretary sat stunned at her desk. Mayor Morales stepped out of his doubled door office to two young women waiting for him but Saivon in her schoolgirl uniform had his full attention. His fixation for young girls was evident as he caressed Saivon's hand while he greeted her, and Sonya fed off of that obsession. Sonya brought Saivon with her on purpose because her counterpart always appeared younger than she really was with womanly attributes and just like that the trap was set. Mayor Morales escorted them into his office and began acquiring why they wanted to meet him,

"So you're trying to start a young assistant's program? The thing is, I already have an assistant and I don't believe we have the funds for a new one."

"Mayor my assistants could help you relieve the stress of your everyday ordeals while your current assistant could deal with the boring city trials of the day. You could call Mayor Lacroix in Chalmette; he'll be happy to enlighten you on our task."

"My stressful everyday ordeals?"

Right then Sonya looked over at Saivon and the schoolgirl uniform-wearing female sashayed over to Mayor Morales sitting at his desk. She dropped to her knees between his legs, unzipped his business slacks, pulled out his semihard phallus and inserted him deep into her wet mouth. The shock on the mayor's face went from surprise to complete pleasure while Saivon's pigtails bobbed up and down as she sucked his manhood into a solid staff in her mouth. Sonya perched herself right on the corner edge of the mayor's desk while she watched with an evil grin. She knew Mayor Morales was falling for her plan but finished the deed off with a binding spell as she exposed her breast to him. With the mayor's head leaning back, Sonya made a small slit across her breast with a razor and squeezed the life fluid into his mouth. Just like with Mayor Lacroix, Dark Spirit slipped from her lips, surrounded them all and engulfed Mayor Morales' soul as a bargaining gift. With a final deep suck on Sonya's succulent nipple, the mayor was under her control and part of her clan.

**7**<sup>th</sup>

## <u>Chapter</u>

Dèsirèe had never been outside of Louisiana for more than a weekend trip to Biloxi with friends so seeing nothing but the open sea was a complete shellshock for her. As much as saving her own life from the fate she saw for her friend Lucas, she feared for her grandfather's safety. She didn't know what to do but she knew she needed to get a message to her last living relative. Dèsirèe pleaded with the seaman that first helped her when she got on the ship and the shipmate was more than happy to help her. She knew just calling Robert-Earl would be a lost cost because the senior citizen wouldn't understand the dangers. Dèsirèe called the only person she had left to trust in the city and that was the Voodoo Priest Baaloo. She tried hard to focus as she dialed the number to the Temple but Dèsirèe truly thought she was losing her mind. Three spirits, Lucas, Felicite and Angelie roamed the large cargo ship like they were part of the crew but Dèsirèe was the only one seeing them. They spoke to her of the urgency of reaching Baaloo and protecting the realm from Sonya's wrath. At the moment the ship's stowaway was only concerned with protecting her grandfather Bobby from being a victim. The phone rang a few times before Baaloo picked up,

"Good afternoon and thank you for calling The Voodoo Spiritual Temple…"

"Baaloo! This Dèsirèe and I really need your help."

"My sister, everybody's looking for you and Trinity. Where are you? What's wrong?"

"Baaloo, whatever they are saying please don't believe it. Sonya tried to kill me at the hardware store. She is beyond dangerous; she has that darkness you always spoke about, deep in her."

"My child, are you safe?"

"Yes, I'm not sure if it's safe to tell you where I am."

"Then don't."

"But please, can you go check on my grandpaw?"

Baaloo assured the shaken Dèsirèe that he would do everything she asked and that her grandfather would be safe. He then asked his voodoo sister about what he heard had happened at the hardware shop. Dèsirèe gave him a detailed story of the Dark Spirit she detected around Sonya and how it would have killed her if it wasn't for Trinity's help. Baaloo started to ask her about "The Light" she felt along with the abilities Trinity showed during the incident. It was hard for her to explain but Dèsirèe knew the Light was there to save her from the evil that surrounded her. When she started to go into detail about what took place at the grave, she was buried in the phone started to static and the call ended. Dèsirèe became frantic as she attempted to call Baaloo back, but the helpful seaman tried his best to calm her,

"It's not you fault. Phone no work well when we in international waters, weak signal."

"International waters?"

"Yes, we are in the middle of the Atlantic Ocean. Come get some rest, we have a long ways to go."

The passenger went with the shipmate to the sleeping quarters because his aura made her feel safe. He overheard her conversation and Dèsirèe could see the concern in his face when he asked her if it was true. Dèsirèe looked over at the three spirits standing in the doorway and they all nodded yes to her, giving the okay to talk freely. She was still trying to understand everything herself but with the guidance from Felicite and Angelie she explained what she was going through. The seaman sat there intrigued in Dèsirèe's story and told her of stories of black magic practices from where he's from. She didn't think the situations were the same but when he explained the details of Asian black magic, Dèsirèe understood. She found a friend in the mariner,

"I've been talking to you all this time. My name's Dèsirèe Glapion. What's your name?"

"Phuc, my name is Phuc Chou."

"I know I ain't hear that right. You said fuck? Like fuck you?"

"No no, no, Phuc with P and H. Phuc Chou."

"My bad."

"You funny."

The three spirits that followed Dèsirèe for days seemed to just fade away into the shadows and left the evacuee with her new colleague. Dèsirèe and Phuc bonded in the sleeping quarters as friends that night, telling stories of their childhood. It was a pleasing change from the ordeal she was going through and an eye-opening experience as she listened to him talk of his family. Phuc Chou lived in New Orleans in a small subdivision deep in the East of New Orleans dubbed "Little Saigon", where most of the Vietnamese Americans stayed. The 38-year-old worked on the cargo ships to provide for his growing family because his wife was pregnant with their first child. Dèsirèe found out that Phuc was running from a past that still had a slight hold on him, but he wanted to change. She could see his heart was caring but he had his own demons he was fighting also. Dèsirèe told him how she was going to school to be a doctor,

"I really don't think any hospital will be hearing, 'Paging Dr. Glapion' anytime soon."

"Being a doctor may have not been in the stars for you. I never wanted to work on a ship all my life, but I am now."

"What you wanna do Phuc?"

"It's too funny. You laugh."

"What? Tell me."

"I want my own grocery store in my neighborhood for my people. Corner stores charge too much and I wanna help my neighborhood."

"You really are a good man, Phuc. Always looking out for people. You will have it; I know you will but we gotta work on a name. It can't be 'The Fuck Store', people gone get the wrong idea."

"Why not Phuc? My name Phuc Chou."

Dèsirèe laughed so hard when Phuc said it out loud and his blank face didn't make it any better because he didn't understand the joke. They relaxed the rest of the night just enjoying each other's company as the ship sailed across the Atlantic.

Right off the shores of the Atchafalaya River, Trinity sat in her well-hidden cabin in the swamps with Eli. The horrific appearance of her friend sitting in front of her was a lot to take in but her compassion for what he was going through pushed her pass mere appearances. Eli's peeling flesh from existing wounds, pus filled infections and the stench of death was all around him, but Trinity only recognized a friend in need. She tried to reverse the spell, but nothing could turn back the damage of death coursing through him. Eli sat there with visions of blood, bone and gore tormenting his mind with no end in sight. Trinity could see the pain on his face as she placed the sharp end of a pocketknife against the thick thread that held his mouth shut. With tears streaming down her face, she freed open the sundried lips of her friend and a gasp of air rushed inside of him. Trinity couldn't understand how a person could do such a thing to another human being. After removing the twine that bound Eli's lips together, Trinity's friend was finally able to communicate with her in words. An unbearable pain came over her when the tortured soul spoke,

"Kill me. Kill me please. I can't do this. I'm already dead, please end me."

Trinity could see the pain surging through Eli but taking his life was not an option she was willing to take. He pleaded with her repeatedly, but she wasn't budging on her decision. Eli couldn't hold back his emotions as a rage rumbled in him. He began flipping fragile furniture over, breaking out windows and shattering a mirror hanging on the wall with one punch. Trinity stood back as her angered friend released his wrath on the wooden shack but as soon as he stepped towards her a magical scene happened. Eli's dark eyes were focused on Trinity as he stomped towards her, but thick vines quickly pushed their way through the floorboards of the shack, wrapping him in a python tight grip. Trinity didn't call on any kind of spirit for help, but it was as if the plant life itself was protecting her. She watched as the thick green vines whipped around Eli, tightening its grip on him, suspending him in mid-air. Trinity didn't want any hurt or harm to come to her friend and reached out as she laid her hand on the vines and the visuals that had been plaguing Eli's head rushed into Trinity's cranium. Screams of pain, blood splatter and graphic dismemberment of body parts invaded the herbalist's mind. She could see what the undead soul was being tormented with, the continuous loop of deadly acts of torture. The flashes of death that were transferred forced Trinity to quickly remove her hand and Eli realized she saw what he saw on a regular. He calmed as he stayed wrapped in the green vines,

"You can see it? You see what I'm going through. Release me from this pain. Please Trinity."

"Eli, I can't."

"Yes, you can."

Trinity fell to her knees because she couldn't bring herself to end a life, even though the life was already nonexistent. The vines released Eli from its hold and as fast as it sprung from the floor it went right back, returning the wood floors back to its original form. The eternal dead soul could see his friend wasn't going to honor his request and let the subject die that day.


Micah found himself hanging upside down in an abandoned farmhouse deep in the woods of Chalmette, Louisiana. His feet were tied together with rope that was strapped to a large wooden beam at the top of the farmhouse. Micah couldn't see much because nighttime had fallen upon the city and the only sounds he could hear came from crickets outside along with the crackling flame in front of him. His mouth was stuffed with an old dirty rag, his hands tied behind his back and shadows moving about pass the flames burning on a stack of logs. Micah knew his life was in danger when the man that he had been knowing and trusting for years stood in front of him as an undead. The zombified Father Toussaint stood there like a watchdog over Micah, lips sewn shut with thick yarn and cloudy white eyes staring forward. The kidnapped knew he wasn't leaving the farmhouse alive, and it was evident when he observed the small table close to him. The table had several knives and blades on it, but a cloth handmade doll wrapped in a torn strip of his clothing lay next to them all. His skull began to pound as blood rushed to his head, but Micah could see a few people standing in the distance in the shadows. He couldn't make them out but then Baka walked up to him with that menacing grin he always carried. The Voodoo Doctor snatched the rag from Micah's mouth,

"You're here today because you need to tell us where Trinity is."

"I don't know where she is."

"Oh, my dear boy, you know. You just don't know you know but Baka will find it. Trust me, Baka can always find what he's looking for."

"Man, get yo sick ass away from me. Help! Somebody help!"

"Scream all you want. Aaaaaah! No one can hear you boy."

Baka picked up a large butcher knife from the small table and Micah just knew his life was over. The Voodoo Doctor slid the blade under the collar of his victim's shirt and began slicing through the fabric, cutting away the clothing. Micah heard a woman shout from the dark,

"Cut them pants off too, I wanna see what my sister's boyfriend working with."

Baka listened and the blade found its way through the jean material, cutting through Micah's clothes with ease. The hanging victim swayed, dangling from the rope that held him, completely naked for everyone to see. The shadows in the dark laughed and giggled but everything went silent as Sonya made her appearance from the dark. She walked up to her kidnapped victim with disgust sprawled across her face as if she was angered at Micah's sight and then she smiled. Trinity's boyfriend didn't know what to make of the situation, confused that a woman he been knowing would have him like this. He begged her to free him and that he wouldn't say anything to anyone about what happened. Sonya continued to smile as she pretended to listen to what she considered groveling from Micah as she glanced over the items on the table. She picked up a boxcutter and extended the blade out as she grazed the blade across Micah's belly,

"You know you can live a few hours with yo guts on the outside?"

"Sonya, I don't know where she is. She didn't tell me anything and I haven't spoke with her."

"You sure? Cause I believe you know something."

"If I knew I would tell you."

"You will. You just don't know it yet."

Sonya took the point of the blade and slowly pushed it into Micah's skin. The hanging innocent tried to hold back his screams because he didn't want to give her the satisfaction of hurting him. She dragged the boxcutter through Micah's flesh, making a six-inch gash across his belly and his blood poured on her hand. The life fluid trickled down into the victim's face as it dripped onto the dirt floor. Saivon rushed over and placed a silver bowl under Micah to catch the blood draining from his body. The torturer wasn't finished as she reached up, grabbing Micah's manhood,

"Oh this little razor ain't gone cut through all this. My little sister took all this dick? Damn."

Sonya wrapped her hand around the handle of a large machete and placed the sharp end against her captive's flesh. She released a smile, her eyes rolled to the back of her head, and she began chanting in a foreign language. Sonya's chanting started to get louder and louder as she sliced into Micah's skin. She sawed through his flesh until the penis was severed from the body and the screams mixed in with the loud chanting. Sonya dropped the phallus in the bowl as if it were a piece of meat for a pet dog. Her deed wasn't done as she dropped the makeshift doll in the bowl too. Sonya then pushed the blade deep into Micah's stomach and pulled down until she hit his ribcage. The gurgling sounds of the victim drowning in his own blood bellowed in the farmhouse while Sonya pulled his innards out for everyone to see. She reached in his chest, wrapped her fingers around his slowly beating heart and pulled it from him. The life that used to live in Micah was no more as the body instantly went limp. Sonya held the heart in front of her, while she finished the last words of her chant and poured the last drips of blood from the heart in her mouth. It felt like electricity filled the barn as Dark Spirit rose from the ground and surrounded Sonya completely. An evil energy surged through her body and she could feel herself getting stronger.

## Chapter

A few days had passed since Micah and Father Toussaint's disappearance but not much was said in the media on the subject. The rash of violent crimes going on in the city had officials occupied and a missing person's report wasn't on the top of their list. Sonya was able to grow her clan right under everyone's noses because of the "Stop the Violence" movement. Neighborhoods were under siege with shootings, robberies and assaults. Citizens were in an uproar of the lack of police presence in New Orleans's rougher areas, asking political officials for help and Sonya saw an opportunity to build. She had New Orleans's Mayor Morales snuggle in Saivon's bosom and controlling him stretched out to city officials. A city councilman along with several other big wigs in the city was next on the upcoming Voodoo Oracle's list and no one was there to stop her. Sonya got Saivon to get the perverted Mayor Morales to set up a secret meeting with a few other mayors. The meeting was a way to get all of them under her control and Saivon whipped up a large batch of gris-gris to spread out to everyone. Saivon's specialty was a mind control gris-gris that if consumed would render the victim helpless to Sonya's orders. Bodily fluids from Sonya were the key ingredients and the sadistic enchantress enjoyed the fact that her victims had a piece of her streaming through their system. Mayor Babineaux of Metairie and Mayor Eddison of Kenner along with Councilman Jackson all arrived at a large mansion on St. Charles Ave. The mansion was recently given to Sonya by Mayor Lacroix whose family owned the massive house for decades. Mayor Lacroix did any and everything to please his dominatrix, including throwing his own blood relatives out on the street for Sonya. Douglas dubbed himself as the concierge to the mansion while Baka was the mansion's designated intriguing escort. They all played their role in getting all the politicians drawn into Sonya's plan, a plan that needed a lot of powerful people under her control.


Over 9 thousand miles from Louisiana, Dèsirèe found herself as a stranger in a strange place but the place was absolutely beautiful and nothing she expected. Being a city girl from New Orleans and never stepping a foot on foreign soil, Dèsirèe was in awe of the Vietnam coast. The docks were similar to what she saw at shipping docks in the city, so it was nothing new, but to observe the amount of people in one place, was astounding. The only time she was a part of that many people walking the streets, was during Mardi Gras. Dèsirèe followed behind Phuc like a newborn puppy following its mother and was not leaving his side. Her Asian buddy found it amusing how she stayed close to him,

"No one gonna steal the little black girl. If anything, they try and sell you some stuff cause they think you rich."

"Who? I'm broke as a joke."

They tracked through a large outdoor market that sold everything from live animals to top tier designer clothes. The market was reminiscence to the French Market back home but on a much greater scale. Dèsirèe's eyes couldn't just focus on one thing as she glanced over the numerous tables and booths. Phuc had called ahead to a few family members that still lived in Vietnam to assist him in finding his new friend a place to stay. He was heading back to the states in a few days and knew Dèsirèe wasn't coming back with him. Finding her a safe place to rest her head was Phuc's main concern at the moment. The arrival of his brother at the end of the market was an eerie reminder of a past he didn't want to think about. Phuc was a member of a very dangerous Vietnamese gang BTK and his connections with the members ran blood deep. He pulled away from gang activity after his wife became pregnant because he wanted a better life for his unborn child. Phuc knew his brother had good intentions but at the same time was a little nervous about his brother's gang affiliations. Tran Chou was a top dog in the gang, but he had a big heart when it came to helping someone in need. Dèsirèe was oblivious to the whole situation but after surviving what she survived, she was willing to take any risk. She hadn't laid eyes on her three ghostly followers in a while, and dismissed the incident as a mental break, believing she made it all up in her head. After being introduced to Phuc's brother, the three of them headed to an apartment Tran had available and Dèsirèe's apparitions showed themselves. Standing at a distance across the street, Lucas and Laveau's daughters just stared at the young New Orleans native. Dèsirèe didn't know what to make of it and her Asian buddy could see the distress on her face,

"It's gonna be ok. My brother take care of you, I promise."

"It's not that. Remember our conversation about the spirits and rituals? Well, I'm seeing those spirits again."

"Some spirits aren't always evil."

"No, I don't believe they are."

"That's good. Maybe they just need you to do something."

"They do but I don't think I'm the right one."

Tran drove two hours to an apartment deep in the middle of the city of Kien Giang District and escorted his brother with Dèsirèe up to the top floor. They showed her around, letting her get comfortable and Tran even had some clothes brought over for Dèsirèe to change in. Phuc told his companion to wait in the condo while he and his brother go take care of some family business. After she knew they were gone, Dèsirèe went straight to the showers and just stood in the middle of the hot cascading waters. As the water washed away her stress like a calming stream, the new Vietnam resident finally had a minute to herself. Tears began to mix in with the showers, a hurt like no other turned her stomach and Dèsirèe fell to her knees crying uncontrollably. She finally pulled herself together and stepped out of the glass shower enclosure to her three familiar entities waiting for her. Frightened back off her feet Dèsirèe tried to cover her nakedness and shouted,

"What da fuck man!"

"When you're ready to talk, we ready to talk."

"Really Lucas? Can you at least turn around?"

"Really Dee? I don't see your physical anymore and what I do see is beautiful."

"Well for me I see a man looking at my butt-ass naked body. Can you please just turn around for me?"

"As you wish my sister."

Dèsirèe tried her best to ignore the presence of the three visitors after getting dressed but Lucas' persistence wouldn't be denied. He made sure that everywhere she went he was right there until she acknowledged them in the room. Felicite and Angelie showed extreme patience when it came to having a much-needed conversation with the Glapion girl but Lucas not so much. He knew the importance of Dèsirèe embracing her purpose and ignoring him was not going to be tolerated. Lucas began describing out loud what Douglas did to him and his brother, how he could feel it all even after he died. He went into detail of how the zombie creator cast him aside after shoving a blade through his heart. Dèsirèe listened with tears in her eyes when Lucas told her how he watched his twin come back to life after getting his throat slit. How Saivon sewed Eli's lips together because he kept making sounds that annoyed her. Even after plea after plea to stop, Lucas made sure to tell his crying friend how he watched them stuff him and her in that wooden crate. Lucas witnessed the evil Sonya and her followers were capable of, but he was confident that Dèsirèe could overpower them if she only believed in herself. Dèsirèe understood she was chosen for some reason, but she had questions and Laveau's daughters had answers,

"What can I do? Sonya is too strong, she almost killed me last time."

"Her strength is in your fear. Dark Spirit feeds off of fear and empowers its host."

"How am I supposed to go up against somebody that has extra help? Why the Spirit of Light left me stranded?"

"The Spirit of Light only helps when you accept your abilities. Your abilities are what you must know first, and Spirit will bless you with unmentionable power. Learn your strengths."

"Ok, learn my strengths, got it. What did Lucas mean when he said he doesn't see my physical?"

Laveau's daughters explained to the curious Dèsirèe how entities don't see the way the living sees. That spirits see the essence of a person, their aura, the purest form of a person. Felicite expressed to the apprentice that spirits can see past the flesh and bone of the living to see who they really are. Angelie went on to tell the pupil how her power of seeing a person's aura is similar to seeing the same way spirits see. In turn that brings her closer to the spirit world which opens another power she would be able to tap into. For the first time since her dangerous encounter with Sonya, Dèsirèe began to embody her voodoo-enriched gifts. Meditating with her three visitors and drawing in on their energy, strengthening herself in return. Pleasure came over Lucas as he witnessed the young woman, he befriended gain the confidence he always had in her.


The meeting Sonya had set up with the political figures started off without a hitch and all of them arrived right on time with thoughts of improving their claims on the city. Some walked in with their chests poked out as if they were the biggest boss in the room, but Sonya knew she was the Queen of the castle. Mayor Lacroix followed behind her like a helpless peasant while Mayor Morales was latched onto Saivon's side with pedophilic intentions running through his mind. The entire group of mayors and powerful individuals all met up in a large conference room where Sonya sat at the head of the table. Senator Elizabeth Patterson was part of the large, invited group of politicians that attended Sonya's meet and greet. Elizabeth Patterson was a New Orleans native that grew up in the rough neighborhood of the Lafitte Projects and fought her way to becoming a politician. The senator had seen every crime imaginable growing up in the 6th ward and she wasn't naïve to the crooked minds of powerful people. Elizabeth thrived on subduing those that fed off of the weak but worked with the same kind of people in order to get what she wanted. She was suspicious of the meeting with Sonya but came to the assembly out of curiosity. Sonya wanted the female politician there because of her powerful influence over a lot of other powerful figures in the city. The room filled with whispered individual conversations as Baka walked in the last few attendees. Senator Patterson was overheard making a comment about the young black girl sitting at the table,

"Who is this high yella gal and why in the hell she got us here?"

"This high yella gal will make you richer than you can imagine, more powerful than you could ever be, respected and feared at the same time. That's why I have you here senator."

"That sounds like a lot of upcoming broken promises dear, and my people need action, not pipe dreams. I came here because you said you could help with the issues going on in New Orleans. If I knew this was some Ponzi scheme, I would have left yo invitation in the garbage where it belongs."

"And that would have been a great loss to you. Especially cause you are struggling with your desires. Desires that are welcomed here with me and all of us. A desire that you hide from the world, but I could empower to the masses."

"My desires? Girl what you talking bout?"

Sonya looked over to Baka standing next to a pair of grand large double doors. He opened the doors to a group of people waiting on the other side, all with a specific gift for all the guests. Senator Patterson knew Sonya knew her secrets as soon as she observed a man along with a woman walk in with a small rolling cart containing straps, whips, dildos and candles. The sight of the couple walking toward her sent chills of anticipation through her body but Patterson held her composure as to not show her excitement. Each one of the visitors in attendance had a companion or more standing behind them but Sonya made sure that she needed their cooperation. The host had drinks and food served to her guests while she went over her plans. Sonya's words flowed over the room like a foggy mist would over a body of water. The visitors believed the young host was just talking to talk but actually she was casting an intricate spell over all in the room. Their eyes glazed over as the spell took hold, their bodies frozen in time and Sonya concluded her ritual with all of them taking a sip of Saivon's special wine. Their control became hers and she treated them all to their elaborate fetishes for unknowingly being her servants. Sonya watched as politicians engaged in sexually driven taboo-type acts right at the table and smiled at the fact that she knew they were all her faithful followers now. The one skeptic that felt like challenging her in the beginning ended up bent over the table giving head to the gentleman of the couple that was sent to her. Senator Patterson had hot wax from a candle poured on her back while the woman of the couple had on a 12-inch strap-on, pushing it deep inside her. The lady of the couple gripped Patterson's ass, trying to push a foot of plastic penis deep in her ass and the senator accepted it all. The male of the couple slapped her in the face with his hardened shaft while he choked her, teasing her lips with his helmet. The senator was in her sexual glory as she got manhandled and ravaged by the couple and Sonya watched it all. Other power figures played with their toys while the host enjoyed the orgy of individuals but then Baka came with some news Sonya had been waiting for,

"I believe we found your sister. I knew that boy was the right one."

"Go get her and bring her back to me, unharmed Baka."

"Yes Queen."

With thoughts of Trinity being back with her, Sonya went back to enjoying her freak fest. The room filled with moans of arousal and smells of sex while Baka left with Douglas in tow. Sonya's tasks were almost complete, and her strengths grew the more people she claimed under her control. To her, it was only a matter of time before she had her sister alongside her, and they could rule all of Louisiana.


Dèsirèe took the gift she was given seriously and studied hard at her craft with prayers along with deep meditations that brought her into other realms. Realms that housed spirits that spoke to her in multiple languages and while in her deep meditation the Voodoo student could understand every spoken tongue. Dèsirèe got to the point where she was able to speak to Phuc and his brother Tran in their native tongue fluently. Tran even introduced their new friend to a few family members, one being their female cousin Bian. The two where the same age but

Bian was a little more street savvy than Dèsirèe and she looked out for her. She also was an underground tattoo artist because getting or owning tattoo equipment was illegal in Vietnam. Dèsirèe was fascinated with the art and became an understudy to Bian. The two became really close when they found they shared some supernatural similarities. Bian was able to see spirits just like Dèsirèe and when the New Orleans girl was caught talking to her three visitors one day, the connection between the two young women became strong,

"You can see them?"

"Yes. I've always seen them in here. I just played like they wasn't here cause I didn't want to freak anybody out."

"I didn't know you could see them too."

"I didn't know you could until I saw you talking to them. That guy watches you all the time."

"Lucas is overprotective sometimes."

"Most spirits are. Most of them just wanna help us in our journey."

Bian thought for the longest she was the only person that was able to see spirits. She hid it from her family in fear that she would be cast out for being a witch. The Vietnamese culture was very leery when it came to the supernatural just like most cultures around the world. The day she noticed Dèsirèe talking with the trio of entities in private was the day a weight was taken from

Bian's shoulders. They shared a secret between one another and Dèsirèe knew her friend could keep secrets being she was a relative to a very dangerous gang. Tran Chou would bring Bian clients to tattoo on the regular and with those clients came numerous packages that were shipped all over Vietnam. Tran was heavy in the narcotics business and the apartment he had for Dèsirèe became a storage area for money along with whatever else he needed to hide away. The two young women stayed to themselves, Bian working as a tattoo artist, training Dèsirèe in the craft and Dèsirèe working hard at her abilities. Abilities that sometimes would show to be beneficial for Tran and Bian at times. Seeing a disturbing aura when a customer comes through kept Tran safe from harm when working with some undesirables. It made Dèsirèe a vital addition to Tran's operation. The more she learned the art of tattooing from Bian the more she was able to apply her supernatural abilities to working with customers. Dèsirèe was able to read her clients, knowing their desires, reading their thoughts, and creating wonderful artwork on them. She enjoyed the craft, and many customers grew to trust the little "da đen" which meant little black girl. Dèsirèe finally found her happy place but the Voodoo understudy was pushed to do more with her craft by the apparitions. Lucas was ready for his friend to do more than just be a human lie detector for a drug lord and a body artist for an underground tattoo shop. Everyday Sonya grew stronger, and he needed Dèsirèe to confront her fears,

"Reading personalities, talking to ghosts and painting on somebody will not help you defeat her. I need you to focus."

"Do you understand the last time I was in front of her, she almost killed me?"

"Are you seriously asking me that question? I'm already dead because of her Dèsirèe! I'm dead! I know you sit here and talk to me like I'm here with you physically but I'm dead. If you don't get a hold of this, so will everybody else. Trinity, your grandfather and countless others."

Lucas' statement hit home and Dèsirèe knew she needed to get back home. Bian became attached to her new friend, not wanting her to leave but understood the circumstances. She offered to travel with Dèsirèe back to New Orleans but fear of losing another friend to Sonya's evil was something Dèsirèe didn't want to chance. Over the next few weeks, the Voodoo student pushed herself further than she'd ever been. Normal meditations that usually only lasted a few hours turned into days as Dèsirèe gained strengths she didn't know she had. The ability to move things with her mind, to summon spirits for protection and countless others. At times Dèsirèe feared what she had learned but then a phone call from Baaloo changed everything for her,

"Hello my sister."

"Baaloo! Is everything ok?"

"For now, yes but I can't be sure that would stay that way. Sonya is growing her following and anyone that challenges her finds themselves erased from the earth, never to be seen again."

"I haven't spoken to my grandpa in a while. How is he? Were you able to find Trinity?"

When Baaloo told Dèsirèe that her grandfather fell very ill she dropped to her knees. To hear the only living family member she had left was nearing death pulled her heart from her chest. To add to her stress Baaloo suspected Robert-Earl's illness wasn't brought on by natural causes but something much worse. Dèsirèe knew she had to get home because Sonya was tampering with her family to get to her. Baaloo also shared a dark family secret he had been hiding from everyone when he told his friend about his twin. A twin he hadn't laid eyes on in years because they chose two different paths in life. When Dèsirèe heard that Sonya's right-hand man was Baaloo's shapeshifting twin brother she couldn't believe the words he was saying. Baka embraced the Dark Spirit that empowered him while Baaloo followed the Light. The Voodoo Priest erased his brother from his life but when he saw him with Sonya, he knew sinful things were strong in them both. He encouraged Dèsirèe to embrace the Spirit of Light and ask it to bless her with its strength. Just like Lucas, he believed Dèsirèe had it in her, the power to overcome anything Sonya could come up with. That night Dèsirèe talked with Felicite and Angelie, desperate for answers. The Laveau girls gave her a history lesson like no other on bad versus evil,

"My child, you aren't the only one that ever had to fight for what is right. These battles have gone on for centuries."

"But why? She was my friend, my sister. We shared everything."

"Our mother went through the same thing. She had to battle with a man she loved. A man that taught her everything she knew."

"Your father?"

"Yes, the man that took our lives and in return she took his. Our father was a very powerful Voodoo worshiper but evil engulfed his heart and his soul. If she could end him, you could do the same."

Dèsirèe fell into a deep trance, pulling in every ounce of power she could, and begged for the Spirit of Light to talk with her. She knew if the Spirit blessed her, she would be able to defeat any adversary she encountered. Spirits after spirits talked to her, blessing her with strengths but never the one she was in search of. The meditation went on longer than ever, minutes turned into hours and hours into days until Dèsirèe gave out from exhaustion. She felt weak, drained and drenched in sweat but the Spirit of Light never approached her. Dèsirèe had come to the conclusion that the Spirit didn't see her worthy enough and gave up but then she felt a warmth come over her. A brightness glowed deep inside as it got brighter and brighter until it filled the room,

"My child, I bless you with all you ask, and it shall be yours. You are worthy."


In the swamps close to the Atchafalaya River, Trinity and Eli lived a life of seclusion from the world but that world came in on them with an evil presence. Animals in the area scattered as if they feared some sort of eminent peril was after them. Trinity's powers tingled with warning and the foliage all around them whispered that danger is coming. She couldn't understand it because she knew no one knew where she was but she could feel something, or someone was near. The air carried a dark electricity in it, the wind blew through the leaves like a lion on the prowl and a low groan crept along the grounds. Trinity placed her hand on a nearby pine tree as it mumbled warnings to her,

"Show me what you see."

Through her mind's sight, the large tree showed her a shadowed image of a man walking towards her cottage through the shallow waters. The man was completely naked, disemboweled with his insides hanging to the ground dragging alongside him and then the man's face came into focus. The sight scared Trinity, pushing her back away from where she stood and shaking her to the core. Eli could see her tremble in fear, and he knew something wasn't right. His sense of self-preservation escaped him because he feared nothing as he stormed through the woods. Snapping pass low branches, splashing through shallow ponds, Eli came face to face with a zombied Micah. Completely under Douglas's control, Micah stared down Eli and only pictured an enemy instead of the friend he used to be. Micah charged toward Eli and their bodies collided with such force it could be heard throughout the swamps. They tussled on the ground like two wild beasts trying to conquer the other. Punches and slaps turned to bites and scratches as they battled one another. Eli's goal was to keep the undead menace away from Trinity but then he seen a glimpse of something much worse. Micah wasn't the only tortured soul tracking through the swamps towards Trinity. A hoard of zombies made their way through the woods in search of one person and one person only. Eli knew he had to get to Trinity before they did but fighting with Micah would slow him down. With strength far beyond any living man, Eli picked Micah up by the throat and impaled his body on a branch extending out from the swamp water. Trinity's friend then ran as fast as he could back to the fishing house where Trinity was, screaming for her to protect herself,

"Lock the doors! Lock the doors, Trinity!"

Eli rushed pass walking corpse, mutated beings that used to be human at one point in their lives, trying his best to get to his friend. The wooden shack came into view and Eli could see Trinity stand on the porch looking for him. He finally got through to her, but the hoard was close behind and nothing, but death filled the air as the fumes of the spirits of the dead pushed through the swamps. Trinity watched the line of undead making their way to her and knew Eli couldn't fight them all off, so she dug deep into herself to protect both of them. She reached down into the earth, with her hands completely covered with mud, branches, and vines as she whispered,

"Protect us. Please protect us now."

The ground rumbled as if there was an earthquake coming, the sounds of birds chirping as they flew away, and the groans of the undead got closer. Then before any of the zombies could take another step a row of trees and thick vines burst through the dirt into a massive wall surrounding the shack. Some of Douglas's creations were gored as the branches shot through the ground, ripping their bodies apart into blood-splattered pieces. The rest found themselves on the other side of an impenetrable wall of trees and vines. They banged their hands against the wall, but it wasn't budging at all and swelled the more they pushed to get by. Creating the wall took a lot out of Trinity as she fell to the ground and Eli carried her inside out of the elements. He could hear the moans and growls coming from the other side of the wall, but he could see Trinity's powers were stronger than he thought. They were safe for the moment, but Eli and Trinity knew that the hoard was just the beginning of something else. With all that was going on Trinity worried about the man in her visions and asked Eli if the visions were true. He couldn't look her in the eyes because he knew it was hurting her to know her love was a part of the undead now. As Eli nodded his head yes, Trinity's cries drowned out the groans from the zombies outside.

9<sup>th</sup>

## Chapter

A month had passed since Sonya introduced herself to the powerhouses that run the city and surrounding cities of New Orleans. She gained some loyal followers and eliminated a few foes in the process. Blood sacrifices in her honor became a reoccurring ritual as congregation members gave themselves and sometimes unknowing victims up to her. The self-proclaimed Voodoo Queen gained a lot of backing when in one night changed the dynamics of the violent crime situation in the city. Just like she did with the politicians, she had a meeting at her house now dubbed Maison Blanche with a few crime bosses of the city. Drug dealers, gang members, pimps and a sloth of undesirables all gathered in the meeting area. Sonya catered to their needs and wants along with casting a spell on everyone in the room. Finding a person's deepest sexual fantasy or infatuation was a gift of Sonya and she used their weakness as her snare to draw them in. With a sip of top-shelf champagne, the entire underbelly of the city was under her control, and no one was there to stop her. After that night the violent crimes seemed to just stop, news of shootings became non-existent and most of the city was in debt to the Voodoo Queen. For all those that did oppose Sonya's reign found themselves as Douglas's loyal undead doing his bidding and raining terror on the weak. Saivon didn't care for all the accolades the Voodoo oracle was getting but she knew saying something would get her killed or worse. Baka followed every word Sonya preached to the letter and no one was above his Queen. He and Douglas continued daily trying to get pass Trinity's barrier spell with the zombies, but every attempt was met with force from the swamps. The Voodoo Queen's little sister's powers were getting frail every day because her supplies were dwindling. Trinity was protected from the beasts outside her fortified walls, but she couldn't get in any food either and she was starving. It was only a matter of time before her walls fell and Douglas's tortured souls entered, dragging her back to Sonya.

Dèsirèe started her journey back to New Orleans but not before traveling to where her bloodline was the riches. It was as if Africa was calling her, and she couldn't decline the call. After numerous attempts not to have any followers, Bian was right there with her. Even though Dèsirèe tried her hardest not to have her friend involved, the tattoo artist was not going to be denied. The two tracked through The Motherland like two tourists, Bian stopping at every available spot to pick up some sort of souvenir. Dèsirèe heard stories of the power of Voodoo in Werst Africa, especially the city of Benin. It was believed that the religion derived from that land and in return declared holy. Dèsirèe walked in open minded to anything she could learn and as soon as she stepped foot in the city a wave came over her. A tingling kind of feeling like goosebumps and electricity flowed through her blood stream as a welcoming. It felt right, it felt like home and Bian could see her friend was absorbing it all. The two found a market near the river where most of the residents sold and traded goods along with stories of spirits. Stories that carried a faith filled appreciation of the religion from the people that followed it. Voodoo didn't carry the taboo it did in the states and even Bian could see the unity it created. As they walked the crowded market Dèsirèe noticed an old man in tattered clothes walking with a cane and what looked like a stray dog at his side. She tried not to pay him any mind as hordes of people walked by but the big smile, he carried with him was enchanting. Everybody except for Dèsirèe ignored the elderly gentleman walking through the market. He wasn't stalking or chasing behind her, but it seemed that everywhere the visitor looked the old man was right there. Bian was busy negotiating with a vendor about a beautiful shawl she really liked to notice the old man but when her friend mentioned him, he vanished. Dèsirèe couldn't figure it out as to where the old man went that fast and just dismissed it while the sights of the city caught her eye. Bian visited other countries before but never Africa and was in awe,

"It is so beautiful out here. It's hot as shit but it's beautiful."

"I know right? This heat is something else."

On the bus ride to Benin, the girls talked to the driver about getting a hotel for the night. For the small amount of money they had to spend, the driver pointed them to a small hotel right on the outskirts of the market. Bian found the hotel pleasing to her eyes because it carried a historical look to it. She loved architecture that embodied a city's history, it kept the culture alive in her opinion. Bian always talked to Dèsirèe about the same factors the city of New Orleans had in that aspect. The buildings, parks and cemeteries had a history there that dates back over 200 years. They both enjoyed the displays of the city's elaborate colors as they made their way out of the market to the front of the hotel. Right when they got close to the hotel's front entrance there was a young woman selling trinkets at a stand in the alleyway. The young woman was in all white, from head to toe, and on her forearm was a tattoo of two colorful snakes intertwined with a palm leaf resting in her lap. She was absolutely beautiful, flawless deep brown complexion, wide light brown eyes, full lips, and a head full of thick, soft natural locks. The trinkets, pendants, and amulets displayed on her stand caught Dèsirèe's eye. The young vendor saw Dèsirèe staring at a silver snake charm that had bright white eyes,

"My father really likes that charm. That's one of his favorites, probably cause it's silver."

"It is pretty."

"You want it? Take it, it is yours."

"Oh no, I can't just take it. How much?"

"No, no. It's a gift from me to you. Papa *Legba* has already welcomed you, the most I could do is give you a gift from me."

"Papa *Legba*? Who is he?"

"My child, you saw him earlier. The old man smiling at you with his lil puppy. He pretty much followed you all through my market."

"Your market?"

Dèsirèe glanced over her shoulder when she asked the question but when she turned back the only thing left was the wooden table all the trinkets were laid out on and the silver charm still in her hand. The young vendor she was just talking to at a completely decorated table of trinkets seemed to have disappeared in a quick second without a trace. The confusion got even more intense when Bian asked her friend why she was just standing in the alleyway like she was talking to someone. Dèsirèe thought she was losing her mind or hallucinating but the charm in her hand was evidence that something had just took place,

"You didn't see that woman selling charms right here?"

"What woman? We was walking to the door and you stopped. I ain't see no woman. Dee, you ok? You might need to get out this sun girl."

"Yeah, that might be it."


Trinity sat quietly in her cottage with Eli meditating on what she could do next while all hell was breaking loose outside. The constant groans and growls coming from the numerous undead on the other side of her protective wall seemed to never end. People who used to be human scratched at the wooden wall and vicious vines snapped at their bodies tearing away flesh. Blood and body parts soaked into the earth as tormented souls tried to enter Trinity's safe place. The continuous battle going on outside pushed the stressed herbalist into a deep self-reflection where she dove deep into herself. It was as if everything around her went away, silence filled her ears, darkness was her only company and Trinity had finally found peace. She's meditated before just to center herself after a hard work-out of her craft but never anything this intense. The dark space brought on a calmness Trinity needed and she began to feel like herself again even though her body was weakening. Right when she released a sigh of relief Trinity's darkness sparked a glowing light, a white light that brightened ever so slowly until it was sunlight bright. From that light, a large tree began to push its way through until it stood right in front of her, majestic in all its glory. The tree resembled something from another world but for some reason, it was inviting to Trinity as it swayed, and the leaves ruffled in the wind that cast across them. She marveled in its appearance but then an old man walked from behind the tree carrying a stick wrapped in red and white ribbon. He smiled at her,

"My child, all isn't lost. I see much strength in you. Strength you have yet to tap into."

Every step he made towards her sprouted an array of green vegetation with colorful butterflies fluttering away. Trinity was lost for words because she never experienced a trance like this before but the old man shared knowledge with her like she's never encountered. Filling her spiritually to the point where she felt energized. Trinity understood the old man as a spirit by the name of **Loco**, the spirit of wild vegetation and guardian of sanctuaries. Her shack in the swamps had become a sanctuary to him and he was there to help her protect it. When **Loco** laid his hand on Trinity's shoulder, he empowered her to defeat the enemies trying to take over her sanctuary. Just as he came **Loco** went away behind the tree and the bright light dimmed until the tree was no more. The sounds of the undead that were banging at her walls began to whisper in the dark until it roared in her ears and Trinity came out of her meditated stated,

"Enough is enough!"

Eli, still set for battle stood at the front door waiting for any intruder to enter but Trinity buzzed pass him as she stormed out. Concerned for her wellbeing Eli chased behind her but the newly enlightened Voodoo herbalist had something in store for her attackers. Just as before, Trinity shoved her hands in the earth and commanded the swamps to protect her from all harm. The forest listened as it rumbled with anger and then like a wave of force, wooden spikes shot from the dirt heading out in every direction there was danger. The massive wall that originally protected them dropped back into the earth, disappearing away and the zombies trucked forward with evil intentions. The wooden spikes that came from the ground pushed towards them literally shredding the tortured souls that were there to harm Trinity and Eli. The wooden spikes left nothing but blood splatter as evidence that they were there and the battle in the swamps was over in seconds. Eli stood there still on edge but every and anything that could endanger them was annihilated. He could see in the distance between the trees Douglas and Baka standing baffled at what they just witnessed. Trinity noticed her sister's goons also and addressed them,

"You can go tell my sister; I'm no longer scared! Tell her what happened here! Send anymore of your undead and the same thing will happen again. This forest is mine, and I am the forest and everything in it."

Sonya's loyal henchmen left the edge of the swamp in fear of their own lives as they headed back to their Queen with news of their failure. Trinity walked back to her cottage with the confidence that no one would come for her again and a wind blew over her as an acknowledgement to that. It was as if she could feel the spirit *Loco* surround her and Trinity took it all in.


Sonya sat in her grand throne in the middle of the large meeting room of Maison Blanche just admiring the number of loyal followers she had acquired. The narcissist couldn't get enough of herself as mirrors throughout the room reflected back at her. Dark Spirit was right there behind her in every image like a shadow encouraging her to perform more and more of her black magic. Her sorcery strengthened her as well as Dark Spirit and an evil pleasure came over them both. While Sonya was being pampered by one of her faithful, Senator Patterson walked in for another one of her private sessions with the oracle. Patterson had become a regular at Maison Blanche because of her guarded fetish, she didn't want the public to know about her and in return she approved every request Sonya could come up with. Laid out completely naked to the world on the cold marble floor, Patterson eagerly waited for her pleasured time with Sonya. The Voodoo prophet began chanting and calling out as a black figure walked from behind her throne,

"***Baron Samedi*** will please your every need Senator. He will turn you inside out til you beg me to stop him. But I will need you to send your people to retrieve my little sister for me. Send them now Senator."

Patterson quickly reached for a phone to call for her private bodyguards to head out to the swamps to meet with Baka and Douglas. The guards were reluctant to go but Senator Patterson's money did all the talking for her. After getting off the phone, the horny fiend parted her legs, as she softly massaged her clit inviting the black figure inside of her. Sonya watched with her usual sinister grin as the dark figure ***Baron Samedi*** devoured Patterson's smoothly wax loving abyss. The Senator reached down to hold onto his head while his devilish tongue vigorously twirled around her clit.

Patterson couldn't believe how fast he got her to her first spastic orgasm as her moistness sprung a leak like a watermain busting under pressure. She squirted out, her juices spraying in *Baron Samedi's* face and his wild tongue licking away the evidence. He sat up on his knees, pulling her close to him as he held the base of his hardened phallus and began to slowly insert himself into her. The massive black appendage, wrapped in thick veins pushed its way inside her, creating an erotic friction against her moist walls. Patterson welcomed every inch of him until it felt like the dick was never ending and she placed her hand against his masculine chest. *Baron Samedi* grabbed her wrists as he held her hands over her head and commenced to pound his way into her. Patterson's moans turned into screams of pleasure as the dark figure pumped his way into her having her second squirting moment of eroticism. The dark figure wasn't finished with her as he turned her over onto her knees and eased himself deep into her tightest hole. He slid in and out of her with no resistance, making his presence known as both hands had a tight grip on her hips. Every thrust of his manhood pushed deeper into her ass until she could feel him in her stomach, Patterson gladly received all of it. Right when she thought *Baron Samedi* would spew out his creamy warmness on her, he puts her in another position to continue his rage on her. The dark figure went from between her legs to between her ass to deep in her throat and back again, every hole was touched. The Senator couldn't take any more of him and reached out for Sonya's help,

"He won't stop. I need him to stop, please."

"Are you sure Senator?"

"Yessss."

Sonya waved her hand and **Baron Samedi** disappeared, vanishing from inside her like a puff of smoke. Patterson flopped on the floor, exhausted from her adventure recalling every moment because she could still feel his girth inside her. Sonya called for her escorts to get the Senator off the floor as her sweaty limp body just fell into their hands. They brought her to one of the many guest rooms so that she could clean herself up and Sonya went back to admiring her own presence.


Bian and Dèsirèe were following the hotel's receptionist to their room when the New Orleans girl couldn't get the incident that happened outside the hotel out of her mind. She kept asking her friend if she really didn't see the woman she was talking about. Bian continuously replied with an adamant no as her answer. Confusion was written all over Dèsirèe's face as she made her way to her room when the receptionist asked her about the incident. The hotel's guest quickly responded,

"There was a lady outside your hotel selling trinkets at a table. The small table right by the alleyway. I was talking to her when I looked away for a second and then she was gone."

"What did she look like?"

"Young woman, dressed in all white, with a tattoo of two snakes on her forearm. Oh, and she had a palm leaf in her lap."

"Oh child, you was talking to *Ayizan*. The *Loa* of the marketplace. She visits from time to time and bless our beautiful market."

"The *Loa* of the marketplace, what's that?"

"In Voodoo, we have different Spirits or Gods for everything. There is a *Loa* for fertility, for the forest, for death and like *Ayizan* for the market."

"There was this old man too that kept smiling at me and she said his name was Papa *Legba*. Said that Papa *Legba* welcomed me in."

"Oh, my child you are truly blessed. Two very powerful *Loa* in one day, yes you are blessed."

The receptionist told Dèsirèe that she was visited by spirits or *Loa* as they are called. The hotel guest listened as the information just flowed from the assistant's lips, not missing one word. Bian wasn't really interested and made her way in the room while the other two stood out in the hall, discussing the Voodoo spirits. Dèsirèe didn't think she would encounter such an experience on her first day stepping into the city of Benin, but she grasped a hold of it all. After their talk the receptionist suggested a visit to a temple in Benin that the visitors may find very interesting. Bian was all game for being a tourist and Dèsirèe wanted answers to her many questions. They went to a nearby restaurant for a bite to eat before heading to the Python Temple. Their table was covered with authentic Benin cuisine. Atassi, a well-seasoned rice & beans, Gboman, a stew and Assrokouin, a wild apple almond sauce, all were devoured by the tourists. After lunch they made their way to the Temple. The Python Temple was a place where the royal python wasn't feared but revered because of the Voodoo religion. Bian was intrigued to see the place because it was said to have at least 100 enormous snakes all roaming the grounds. Dèsirèe on the other hand wanted to go to the Temple because of its spiritual factors. Benin had become a welcoming place to her, and she started to feel its energy. Dèsirèe's three stowaway entities could see she had come into her own with her gifts and their presence became less and less in Benin. She didn't want to see Lucas and Laveau's daughters leave but they encouraged her growth and let her know they were no longer needed,

"You found that spirit deep in you, don't ever let it go and you will be just fine."

"Lucas, you been with me since the beginning of all this."

"And I'll be there with you always. Just not how you would imagine me to be."

"I don't wanna let y'all go."

"My child, you have all the tools. ***Bondye***, smiles on you."

Before Dèsirèe could ask one more question or make one more comment they were gone. She couldn't feel their presence or sense any of their energy and the newly orphaned soul wept in what she felt as a loss. Bian could sense the exit from the three entities too when she asked her friend what happened. Dèsirèe's saddened explanation could be felt in every word she spoke, and Bian listened to her friend but at the same time spewed the same words Lucas told to her,

"You'll be fine. You got this girl."

The two walked up to the Python Temple and their imaginations were no match for what they witnessed. A large ten-foot wall surrounded the place with two large metal doors to the main entrance of the Python Temple. The walls and doors were painted in bright brilliant colors, drawings of snakes and other figures adorned the area but when the two entered the temple the sights were amazing. A guide welcomed them in, showing them a small market where there were all types of African art, masks, and trinkets. Dèsirèe's eyes darted back and forth across table after table of all sorts of artifacts. Bian immediately went to a table that carried hand-carved dolls of all sizes,

"Is this Voodoo dolls?"

"My Asian child, please don't confuse this with what the white man made up for you."

The vendor went into detail telling Bian about what the carved figures were and what they meant, educating her on the religion. Dèsirèe took the opportunity to venture deeper into the temple and came across a clay house that had a large wooden door with two snakes carved into it. When she stepped closer to the house the door opened with a man holding a seven-foot python on his shoulders. Shocked at the sight but far from scared Dèsirèe walked towards the man and he placed the large serpent on her shoulders. The animal's cold skin was like a cooling to her, and its squeeze was like an embrace from a close cousin. Dèsirèe felt oddly welcomed in the temple after receiving the serpent and walked around with the snake on her shoulders. The snake handler told her the snake's name was Zombi and he was one of his largest in the temple. Dèsirèe discovered that Zombi is another term for **Damballah**, which was a Voodoo **Loa** that resembled a serpent and when the snake nuzzled at her pocket the other tales became true. She reached in her pocket to pull out the silver charm **Ayizan** gave her, and the animal just gazed at the charm as if he was admiring it. Curious with her usual questions Dèsirèe asked,

"So **Damballah** the serpent god is **Ayizan**'s father?"

"There's only one God my child, ***Bondye***. But yes, ***Damballah*** is the serpent ***Loa,*** and he is the father to ***Ayizan***, you know your Voodoo child."

**10**<sup>th</sup>

## Chapter

With a newfound strength, Trinity roamed her domain in search for any left-over zombies in the swamps. She caught a few stragglers walking through the marsh and with devastating accuracy from whipping vines beheading the tortured souls where they stood. Trinity had become accustomed to only having one undead soul in her presence and Eli was there as her helping hand. They cleared out the swamps of the unwanted guest and began to make their way back to the cottage. Edible berries, fruits along with various vegetation seemed to line their way back to the shack and Trinity couldn't help but to snatch some up for her dinner. Being a part of the undead Eli had no desire for food and just talked to Trinity as she picked through the vegetation,

"I want to apologize for asking you to end me when I first came to you. That was selfish of me and I'm sorry I put you in that position."

"Eli you were desperate, and I understand. It's not called a tortured soul for nothing, and I can feel your pain. I care for you; I love you and we gone get through this."

"I love…"

Before Eli could finish his sentence, a loud boom was heard, and his head exploded with so much force that his brain matter splattered in Trinity's face. She fell to the ground in complete fear as Eli's body seemed to just drop where it stood, and gunfire darted through the forest. With her friend's body lying next to her, Trinity peered through the trees and discovered a group of armed men making their way towards her. The combat gear wearing terrorist had their rifles pointed forward as they carefully walked through the swamps toward Trinity. Her fear escaped her, and anger filled her spirit as she commanded the marshlands to fight back. The ground rumbled as if an earthquake was coming, and the hitmen looked terrified at how the forest around them came alive. Small ponds rippled and bubbled while leaves fell from the sky and birds took flight. Large trees began to move as if they were walking, branches reaching out and snatching their victims up into the canopy with only blood trickling down as a remainder of them. The men tried to shoot at anything moving but it had no effect on the things coming at them. Bright green vines whipped from every direction, pulling the henchmen's attention, disarming them at the same time. Black water moccasins snapped at any visible skin, leaving their venom to course through their bodies. Wild boar charged, goring their victims in submission, and alligators fed on the gunmen as they pulled them into the deep. Their screams were muffled by the land. The swamp listened to Trinity's cry for help and answered with tremendous force as the last two men retreated out of the forest to a black Suburban waiting for them. Her protection was evident there and it was going to take a lot more than a few mercenaries to take her out. Once Trinity recovered from the attempted assault on her, she focused on her deceased friend still laying in the same spot he fell. She said a prayer for Eli's spirit to finally have peace, then the earth opened up and took him in. Even the animals around looked as if they mourned the loss Trinity was having and they followed her back to the shack as escorts. Walking through her door without her friend behind her was a torment Trinity wasn't ready for and the tears flowed like the Atchafalaya. Pain riddled her body as she fell to the floor weeping from Eli's second death. The thought that her sister was behind it all flooded her mind and Trinity boiled with hatred for her own blood,

"She has to be stopped."

Images of what happened to Eli, the silhouette of the man who used to be Micah and numerous souls she had to end because of Sonya all came rushing in. Trinity had had her fill of the entire situation, and she was ready to end her sister's reign of terror. She just needed the confidence to accomplish it because Trinity feared she wouldn't take the opportunity to kill her sister if she could.


The mayors of the surrounding cities held their weekly meeting at Maison Blanche, and they invited Governor Edwin Baptiste this time. The Governor heard rumors of the underground activities that went on at Sonya's gatherings and curiosity took over. He was a third-generation political figure in his family, with a boisterous attitude of power about himself but Baptiste also had a sadistic nature too. Behind closed doors the Louisiana Governor enjoyed beastly acts on frail individuals that were intimidated because of his power. The stories that anything is accepted in Maison Blanche was tantalizing to him and the hardened bulge in his custom-made slacks was evidence that he was ready for Sonya's adventures. Governor Baptiste walked in the grand foyer as Baka greeted him,

"Governor Baptiste, welcome to Maison Blanche."

"The French White House huh. What does Maison Blanche have to offer me?"

"We offer everything you desire Governor."

Baptiste released an evil grin as he doubted the reply Baka gave him. The Governor followed the escort to the main hall where a few other dignitaries along with a few undesirables waited for Sonya's arrival. The top dog wasn't used to having to wait for someone and appeared agitated to what he considered an inconvenience. Two very large muscular men dressed in only a cloth covering their lower half pulled at the double doors of the community room. The guest clapped at the appearance of Sonya walking in greeting everyone with a smile as Governor Baptiste huffed at how the crowd was excited to see her. He had never been in her presence before and wasn't impressed at what he considered to be a sideshow act. Baptiste didn't believe in the whole voodoo thing and found it to be a parlor act at most. He stood there watching Sonya weave through the crowd of people until she stood right in front of him,

"Governor Baptiste, thank you for joining us."

"I wasn't gonna come but Mayor Lacroix and Senator Patterson ensured that I would enjoy my time here."

"All my guest enjoys their time here Governor. I personally make sure they do."

"Oh, so if I'm not satisfied…"

"I will definitely satisfy your pleasures."

"Well let's get the party started."

"The party has already begun."

Sonya raised one hand, snapped her fingers twice and the two large guards opened the double doors again to another large group of people that mingled in with the VIP's. The hostess caressed the Governor across his manicured beard, smiled and told him to enjoy himself as she walked away. The cocky politician noticed a challenge in Sonya he wanted to accomplish but right when he went to step to her a young woman in a business suit reached for his hand. Baptiste had never seen the woman before, but she knew everything about him though. She named off all his credentials as if she was reading from his resume, he found it cute, but he wasn't impressed. Baptiste's attention was caught when the young woman began calling out names, and names of sexual partners. Names that only he knew who they were, and the young woman smiled when she discreetly mentioned some of their favorite sexual positions. The Governor was drawn into the woman's words like a moth in a spider's web and she spun out more words that enticed him to a sensual aroused state. The young woman walked Baptiste through an orgy of sexual encounters occurring throughout the grand room to a private room for them. His bodyguards followed close behind, but the politician waved them off. Once inside the room, the woman immediately began fastening wrist restraints to herself that were hanging from the ceiling. Baptiste looked at the items laid out on a nearby table. Leather whips, wooden paddles, feathers, razors and an array of sexual paraphernalia all lined up perfectly for the choosing. The devilish grin the young woman let loose was accompanied with her forwardness,

"I forgot to disrobe so I'm a leave that for you to do."

"You sure you want me to do that?"

The young woman released a moan of anticipation as the Governor picked up a large bowie knife and he began slicing through her blouse. The razor-sharp utensil went through the clothing like hot steel on warm butter, revealing her laced bra. Governor Baptiste was a professional at the fetish of S&M and found more pleasure in inflicting pain than the pleasure of the act. The room oozed darkness as the only light it carried was from the collection of wax candles all around. The heat from the flames created somewhat of a hotbox and sweat began to drip from the young woman's brow as Baptiste caressed her skin with the blade. He then slid the knife between the waistband of her skirt and her skin, slicing through the cloth with ease. Her matching lace panties underneath revealed a plump mound of pussy the Governor couldn't help but to grab a handful of. His young victim squirmed in his hands as she dangled from the restraints that held her and Baptiste joyed in the fact that she couldn't run from him. He reached for one of the candles, dripping hot wax against her soft skin and his fingers found their way inside her decorative bottoms, massaging her clit. Right when the Governor's attention drew him to a leather whip waiting for him on the table, the door slowly creeped open. Sonya entered the private party to Baptiste subjecting the vixen to his onslaught of pains with all the available toys he had to play with. The hostess watched as the Governor administered his erotic victim with brisk slaps from the leather strap clinched in his fist. The loud cracks from the short whip were only muffled out because of the shouts the young woman let loose from her lips. Baptiste realized Sonya was watching his performance and he wanted to glorify his dominance as he wrapped one hand around the woman's neck. He squeezed so tight that her skin reddened under the pressure as the victim gasped for the air escaping her. Still with his hand latched around her neck, the predator aggressively rubbed the leather whip between the young woman's thighs. Thinking he was impressing Sonya with his acts, looked over his shoulder to find the Voodoo Queen nonchalant with the show, puffing on a small tobacco pipe. Sonya blew smoke rings in the air as she expressed her disinterest,

"That was cute."

"Cute?"

"Yeah, cute. I'm a need a little more from you to get my attention."

"You want more?"

"Hell, look at her. She wants more. I want both of you to give me your all."

Baptiste turned back, looked the young woman in her eyes and was caught off guard when the vixen spat in his face as if she was angered with him for not performing. The Governor wrapped both hands around the woman's neck, attempting to squeeze the life out of her for disrespecting him in such a way. She moaned under his pressure as she caressed his leg with her foot, her eyes begging him for more. The young harlot's actions turned Baptiste on greater than he had ever been because usually, the women are pleading for him to stop but this one wanted more from him.


7,200 miles East of New Orleans, Dèsirèe's journey through the African plains brought her across a nation of people who believed in the faith she was still a little confused on. The people took her in as a sister, teaching her everything they knew, showing her things she could never find in any book. It all allowed her to hone in on her gifts, making her stronger every day and opening her eyes to what the Voodoo Spirits wanted from her. Dèsirèe found herself enthralled in the religion that carried a wicked rumored background back home and some of the natives even clarified some rumors. The walking dead, curses, possessions, poisonous spells and a collective of a lot of darker magic plagued the good of the religion.

Growing up the way she did had her in constant conflict with what she felt was the right way and what she was witnessing. Visits from ghostly figures, welcoming her into the realm, became a norm, and complex visions invaded her mind on a regular. Some days Dèsirèe didn't know if she was dreaming or wide awake because everything was so vivid. She had times when she would hold a full conversation with someone, only for them to disappear in a puff of smoke or walk away vanishing in front of her eyes. The old man from the market, now compassionately known as **Papa Legba**, was one of her frequent visitors. **Papa Legba** would always have a message for Dèsirèe from her friend Lucas, encouraging her every time. The creator **Loa** and father to the marketplace goddess **Ayizan**, began to make his presence known to Dèsirèe on occasion also. **Damballah** fondly known as the serpent god was far from any human form Dèsirèe had ever seen. Resembling a huge python, similar to the ones pictured at the temple in Benin, **Damballah** was extremely kind to her and only hissed but his eyes spoke volumes along with great understanding. Other **Loa** like the gentle barefoot farmer **Zaka**, came with whispers of gossip about people all around the Voodoo apprentice. **Zaka** was entertaining to Dèsirèe because he appeared as a young man close to her age, full of energy, lively and always willing to talk,

"Girl, why you scared?"

"I'm not scared **Zaka**."

"Hmm, seem scared to me. That other girl not scared at all."

"What other girl? You mean Bian?"

"No, Bian fun. She likes me, I know she do, and I like her too. I'm talking bout that Sonya girl. You know she did nasty with my brother Baron? *Baron Samedi* always doing nasty things with her, making her stronger. You strong but you scary."

*Zaka* would always drop a little gossip then dart off into mist, leaving Dèsirèe to her own conclusions. His words would always leave a bad taste in her mouth because the New Orleans native doubted herself constantly, but she also knew what she needed to do. Hours of meditation brought her into what she could only describe as outer worldly with all sorts of Spirits. Dèsirèe found herself sometimes as the visitor and not the visited during her recent meditation sessions. Her powers grew to the point where instead of Papa *Legba* meeting her in her own world she was meeting him in his. The old man *Loa* would share mysteries, warnings and stories of past practitioners that were just as powerful as she was. Dèsirèe asked him about the mysterious lady Marie Laveau that would come in her dreams before she knew anything about "the faith". *Legba* would laugh,

"Your concerns are you and not your ancestors."

"But my ancestors are what brought me here."

"Your ancestors only woke you up my child. It's up to you to open your eyes so you can see."


Dèsirèe would take in *Legba's* words just the same as she did with the gentle farmer Spirit *Zaka*. She went from being a tourist in Africa to becoming a regular with the citizens of Nigeria. The residents would refer to her as the black American girl who speaks Vietnamese and Yoruba, a common language in Nigeria. She built up a good clientele by learning their language along with their culture. Dèsirèe along with Bian continued to practice the art of tattooing because it brought in money for them. Their craft was totally illegal in Vietnam, but they did it anyway and nothing changed while they were in Africa. Customers would come from all over to get some sort of artwork from the Voodoo practitioner because sometimes she would have a vision while giving someone an artistic piece. Maybe it was from the physical contact of the tattoo needle or just the close encounter with the person, but the artist could see their ambient air clearly. Dèsirèe's ability to read auras grew to a magnitude where she could see a person's past, present and glimpses of their future. With help from her partner Bian, they stayed with a customer coming to their spot to receive a tattoo and maybe have a reading too. Bian understood how important the whole process was for her friend and for the first time didn't see her own gift of being able to see

Spirits as a curse. The Asian tattoo artist didn't speak to Voodoo Spirits like her partner because she didn't carry that gift but on occasion a deceased family member of a customer would visit with a message for them. The duo's makeshift tattoo shop, close to the marketplace, had become a regular spot for many to visit, pray, chant and just embrace the faith of Voodoo.

Back at Maison Blanche in the secluded sex chamber Sonya had set up for Governor Baptiste, they continued to enjoy the erotic escapades with the tied-up vixen. Baptiste turned up a notch as he whipped the young woman with a six-foot leather whip across her bare back. The woman's screams seemed to arouse Sonya and the Governor as her pain became their pleasure. Baptiste loved the idea of inflicting all sorts of agony on his victim and Sonya encouraged him to do more with every move. The restrained woman looked as if her body couldn't take any more of the Governor's attacks but then Sonya stepped in with a whispering spell to her ear. The young woman looked as if she was in a trance as her eyes rolled back only revealing the whites of her eyeballs. The Voodoo Queen turned to a heavy-breathing Baptiste as the sweat trailed down his forehead and blew a white powder in his face,

"Do my will and spill her blood for me."

Sonya's words seem to have taken over Baptiste's body and he picked up a thin razor blade. He couldn't resist sliding the blade across her chest, slicing open her flesh releasing her blood as it dripped down her breast. The Governor dropped to his knees in front of the woman, putting one of her thighs on his shoulder and burying his head deep between her legs. As his tongue found its way to her pleasure pocket, he licked her throbbing clit, tasting all her juices. He continued to slice on her skin with the razor, opening new wounds that continued to pour blood out of her. Sonya indulged herself in the activity as her hand slid through the young woman's life source and she wiped her palm across the Governor's forehead. The handcuffed victim no longer felt the pain she was being put through as she gave herself up to Sonya, who dug into the wounds Baptiste made. The Voodoo Oracle began chanting in foreign languages aloud, the room rumbled as a wind blew across the walls and the flames on the numerous candles flickered. The dark spirit **Loa Baron Samedi** arose from the floorboards in a black mist, stood behind the young woman and snatched her head back. **Baron Samedi** handed Sonya a black curved dagger,

"Spill her blood for me now and gain her life force."

Sonya pushed the point of the dagger through the woman's throat until it sliced it completely open, and blood poured out like a river. The

Voodoo Queen drained the woman dry, like a vampire as she drank the blood and Baptiste continued his sadistic oral pleasures until the young victim went limp in his mouth. Covered in the woman's blood, the Governor was pushed to the floor by Sonya who mounted his still hardened manhood. The two engaged in a blood thirsted filled erotic act as Sonya grasped hold of the base of Baptiste's dick and guided it deep inside her,

"Yea, right there. Get in there Governor."

While he licked the still-fresh drips of blood off her areolas and enjoyed her warmness wrapping around his stiffened phallus, the sounds of sex filled the atmosphere. The room became humid like a sauna as the walls began to sweat, Sonya slid slowly up and down as the Governor gripped her soft round ass. The hardened shaft seemed to push its way deep inside the Voodoo seductress as each pump brought on an ecstasy-induced euphoria. The two were so into pleasing one another that they failed to see **Baron Samedi** still standing there in his dark ghostly form. Being the Spirit of Death, **Baron Samedi** plucked the hanging victim's soul from her body, pulling it down with him through the floorboards and they disappeared. Once they were gone, Sonya could feel a glow inside her, a growth of strength, and just as promised **Baron Samedi** gifted her more power. The slow grind her and Baptiste were wrapped in turned into a vigorous fuck until the Governor couldn't hold out anymore. He whimpered and shivered as Sonya siphoned out every creamy ounce of him. They collapsed to the floor, exhausted from their rigorous session but laughing at the same time. Baptiste stood from the floor and helped his Oracle up as she suggested he go clean up before leaving the room,

"You might wanna go wash all that off. Can't have you walking out filthy."

"What about the girl?"

"No worries my dear, my men will take care of the shell hanging there."

"Shell?"

"Oh yes, she is no longer there but that is no concern of yours. We have much to discuss my dear. Much to discuss."

One of Sonya's guards escorted the Governor to the showers, and she left in the opposite direction pleased with herself. Her plans of domination were coming together as whispers of spirits and demons echoed down the halls.

## Chapter

Trinity's secluded lifestyle began to bring on a hermit-like mentality as she warded off any and all intruders. It became an unspoken rule to local fishermen and hunters to avoid the area completely in fear of the urban legend in the swamps. Small boats were capsized by mysteriously protruding branches from the water and camouflaged attire-wearing men were chased out the woods by angered animals. All of them told tales of seeing a young black woman dressed in vines standing close by with bright green eyes shouting for them to leave. Trinity had charted off a few acres of land that was solely hers and no one dared enter it without her approval. The Swamp Queen had made a stern statement along the Atchafalaya River that she was the only one to roam its grounds. She still mourned the loss of Eli daily and visited his gravesite on the regular just talking to him as if he was still there with her,

"Today was a rough one. That big alligator you never liked caught one of the hogs off guard at the edge of the pond. I can still hear his squeals in my head. But it's all part of the life cycle, someone has to die to feed another. Talk to you later…love you."

Trinity spent hours meditating, drawing in strengths from the **Loa Loco** and the Spirit of vegetation blessed her abundantly. The wetlands dweller always had food on her table, a safe place to sleep and plenty of quiet days to reflect. The only thing about Trinity reflecting was that it brought on a hatred for her own blood and getting back at Sonya started to become a priority.


The city of New Orleans' Voodoo Queen had her fingers deep in the pockets of several prominent men in the city and surrounding areas. Her name was on the lips of everybody who lived in her domain, from the ones that held her atop of everyone and the ones that feared her presence. Sonya finally felt the power and strength the Dark Spirit promised her on that night. Governor Baptiste used his political powers to appoint her as the city's ambassador and all the elected officials agreed. The oracle relished in the newly received power with a celebratory event at Maison Blanche, where all the wealthiest gathered in her honor. The estate ran hot with a sexual tension and the hostess held back no punches as neighborhood drug dealers rubbed body parts with esteemed business personnel. It was an orgy of elites, undesirables, and the everyday common worker in attendance. The dark *Loa Baron Samedi* roamed the grounds like a lion in search of his next soul to seize. Sex wasn't the only thing up for service as some of the guests pleasured themselves in sadistic rituals of black magic. The chanting along with dancing brought about another *Loa* in Maison Blanche and Sonya found him very familiar. The Dark Spirit she met in her mirror on that fateful night resembled the *Loa* that aggressively prowled the mansion. The *Loa Kalfu* was the twin of Papa *Legba*, but they were total opposites and the evil-spirited *Loa* thrived in all that was wrong in the world. Where *Baron Samedi* enjoyed every erotic act the human race engaged in, *Kalfu* appreciated the darkness mortals brought about. Pain, anguish and all sorts of detriment was his vice. The small group that called *Kalfu* up front found themselves wrapped in cutting sessions, strangulation and so much more on one another along with giving themselves up to his will. The *Loa* laughed as women along with men offered their bodies to him in exchange for power and glory. It was as if they were making a deal with the Devil and none of them resisted the urge. Sonya could see *Kalfu* was enjoying the festivities as she greeted him,

"Thank you for coming."

"For coming? I've always been here. I just needed a reason to show my face."

"Would you like a drink my Lord?"

"Rum bitch."

Sonya became a servant in that quick second and knew not to question the powerful *Loa* that stood in front of her. She knew just as he granted her all that she had he would take it all away too. The Voodoo Queen handed the Dark Spirit his drink and went back to hosting her party. The brutal and perverse began to bleed into the erotic as patrons went from sensuous pleasures to viciously pleasing their ferocious side. The lude eroticism of **Baron Samedi** started to dim and the evil spirits of **Kalfu** grew stronger. The crowd cheered for a sacrifice and Baka along with the zombie maker Douglas brought Sonya a drugged induced volunteer to center stage. Saivon stood in the background as she watched with envy all the accolades the self-proclaimed Voodoo Queen received. The dark potion producer knew it was her gris-gris that seduced the masses and not Sonya, but no one acknowledged her works. Saivon watched as the audience wowed at the fireworks the Voodoo oracle put on for them. Her malice for the woman she used to look at as a friend grew to hatred because of what she felt was disrespect to her craft. Small sprinkles of gunpowder over open flames brought on a fireball show for all who witnessed Sonya's performance as she charmed the drugged victim swaying in front of her. Commanding the woman to rip her clothes from her body as she seemed to be under the

Voodoo witch's trance only encouraged the audience to want more. Some of the men carried a long table in front of Sonya and stretched the woman on top of it as the Queen continued her erratic chants. Through the crowd, Sonya could see *Kalfu* smiling at what would come next and she didn't disappoint her Dark Spirit. The same curved dagger she used before found its way in Sonya's hand again. She slid the sharp utensil down the woman's body, from her throat to her navel and sliced the victim open with ease. Blood bubbled to the surface, pouring out like an overflowing river onto the table and then the floor. Sonya reached down into the woman's abdomen, deep red fluids covered her forearm and she fished around until she found what she was looking for,

"There you are. C'mere my pet."

The crowd all gazed as the life left the woman lying on the table in front of them but then cheers and chanting erupted through the mansion. The crowd couldn't believe what they were seeing, and Sonya's performance continued to amaze them all. The Voodoo Queen pulled a five-foot-long, black and bloody python from out of the deceased woman. The demon-like serpent hissed and snapped at everyone around as it glanced over the crowd of people stunned at the sight of it. Sonya announced the soul of the woman was deep inside the creature and the audience chanted Sonya's name as their Queen. Throughout Maison Blanche, people were all in awe of the magical feat Sonya produced but Saivon only saw a well-managed parlor trick for the naïve. She was done with what she felt was disrespect to her art and no longer wanted to work with the Voodoo Queen or her large following. Saivon knew she needed a way out and moving in silence was her only option.

Dèsirèe traveled across most of West Africa, honing her crafts in tattooing and her psychic readings. The newly appointed Benin medium acquired a great deal of respect from the natives as a very powerful "mambo" or Voodoo Priestess, as it was called. Dèsirèe's powers only grew stronger every day the more she practiced and with the encouragement from the people along with Bian she had a lot of practice. Her Vietnamese counterpart, Bian, was like a spiritual businesswoman when it came down to finding clients. Even though the young Asian girl was somewhat an outsider to them, the African community took her in as one of their own. From learning their culture, speaking their language, and taking part in their religion, Bian became one of them. Being a sidekick to Dèsirèe wasn't something she thought she would be when they first started out on their journey, but she embraced and enjoyed every bit of it. She would always clown around with her friend when clients would come through for a tattooed reading,

"Queen Dee, your 10 o'clock is here. Would you like a cup of tea, bissap juice or a glass of Sodabi?"

"Girl, you play too damn much. Just let them in."

"Yes ma'am. You sure you don't want any Sodabi? I'm a make me one."

"Really Bian? Who drinking liquor at 10 in the morning, besides you?"

"Shit, it's 12 somewhere."


Sodabi was the Beninese people's vodka version of liquor, mostly used for special occasions along with religious engagements like Voodoo services and Bian's new favorite drink. Dèsirèe dabbled in the beverage but her friend always made sure to have a drink or two on standby. The Vietnamese native sometimes needed a buffer for the extraordinary acts that occurred during Dèsirèe's sessions. As a child, Bian was always able to see the spirits of people who passed on and even talked to them sometimes but the psychic meetings her friend would have, were on another level. Items moving around on their own was a norm to her but possessions, visions and physical touches from the unknown were a bit much. The neighborhood mambo's powers grew so much that when spirits and entities would visit it would be a barrage of ghostly figures from another realm. Dèsirèe was able to open the spirit realm with her mind like a person would open the door to a house but just like Papa *Legba*, she was the guardian to that door also. She could control what came through, who could speak, draw energy from her clients or the energy of the spirits visiting and even use that energy in the mortal realm. Dèsirèe became a very powerful clairvoyant in a sense, pulling from her gift became a gift in itself because at times very hateful spirits tried to make an entrance. Powerful *Loa* like *Jean Petro*, *Baron Samedi* and *Kalfu* with his plethora of demons all would try to enter Dèsirèe's sessions, but she would deny them all. Sometimes catching them off guard that a mere mortal was strong enough to revoke them access,

"You deny me child? Do you know who I am bitch?"

"Not today Devil. Not today."

"I will eat your soul in a beef soup."

"You can't touch me unless I let you. Be gone Devil."


Dèsirèe knew who she wanted in and who she wanted out in order to perform clear-minded for her patrons. Hellish *Loa* like *Kalfu* brought nothing but hatred and detest to everything that was holy about her works and his presence brought on a dèjà vu in a sense. Dèsirèe couldn't pinpoint where she recognized the angry *Loa* before, but his dark presence seemed too familiar

to her like she had been face to face with him
before. He along with a few others were pretty
much banned from entering any of her sessions
with clients. Dèsirèe prided herself on the fact
that all of her customers would have pleasant
meetings with her, no matter how bad the
situation.

**12<sup>th</sup>**

## Chapter

The year 1994 rolled over to '95, time had
seemed to fly by for everyone, and the clock

wasn't slowing down one bit. Mardi Gras came and went through the city like a whirlwind, festival after festival, joyous moment after another and the underbelly of the state thrived. Sonya's reign as Voodoo Queen wasn't stopping either and all that stood in her way were mowed down like a thin blade of grass. Politicians along with neighborhood goons all prayed to her to grant their greedy natures with numerous amounts of wealth and power. The Voodoo Oracle had her people wrapped around her pinkie and she gloated at the fact she had so many followers. Trinity on the other hand was content with her surroundings but the sour stench of her sister's regime was an irritating bother. The secluded herbalist would hear whispers on her ventures through the swamps. Ghostly chats between Spirits roaming the grounds of a powerful being stretching across the land taking up any and all weakened souls. Trinity knew it was her sister they were speaking of and one half of her just wanted to end Sonya's life, but the other half still had love for her, only family member. The Paris girls were orphaned as teenagers when both of their parents were killed in a botched robbery at their family's convenience store in the 7th ward. In the eyes of the state, Sonya who was 17 at the time was old enough to take care of them both so they avoided being placed in a foster home. Having to grow up fast drove both of them to better themselves but for Sonya, it drove her to want more and that wanting turned to a greed in a sense. Maybe it was seeing someone take something precious from her that was the driving force for her to take from everyone else. Or maybe it was just a deep-seated emotion that needed something traumatic to bring it out of her. Either way, Sonya was deep into the darkness that surrounded her and clung to it all like a vice grip. Trinity took another course in life where she fed on the good in the world, inspiring and nurturing it like a newborn baby. Her gift of bringing new life into the world like a newly growing bud of a rose was like a light but her gift was shadowed by Sonya's darkness. Trinity knew she had to meet that darkness with her own scale of shadows. Her shadows came in the form of storm clouds over the city of New Orleans as Trinity called on the numbered of *Loa* in control of it,

"Great *Agwe* lend me your strength. You are the Shell of the Sea, and your powers of rain is needed. I call also Sogbo and Badè for your gifts of lightning and wind. I call for storms to rain down onto the unjust, on the oppressors and those surrounding my sister. Grant me this gift on the 5th month of nineteen and ninety-five."

The sky opened to a downpour on the city, a full month before hurricane season even begun and everyone, even meteorologists were caught off guard. Dark gray clouds rolled through New Orleans, releasing everything they had onto the city and the rains looked as if they weren't stopping. Canals along with bayous overflowed, streets flooded, trees broke under the pressure of the storm and people were stranded like prisoners in their own homes. Sonya could feel the disturbance wasn't natural and could feel Trinity's presence in the raindrops,

"I see you've gotten stronger baby sister. This won't stop anything though, mere kid games."

Sonya called for her faithful servant Baka to talk to Saivon about a counterattack on the storm beating at their doorstep. Lightning crashed and thunder rumbled through the streets as water filled every roadway, turning New Orleans into a city in a lake. 130 miles away from where the great storm poured down on the city, Trinity stood at the banks of the Atchafalaya River drawing in every bit of the *Loa* in control of the downpour. She stood there like a statue with her arms stretched out to the heavens, winds circling around her like a small tornado, and every animal near scrambling for cover. Over her, there wasn't a cloud in the sky, but rumbles could be heard for miles. Trinity's request was granted with all the *Loa* she called on and she was pleased with the visioned results that were shown to her. After getting word from Baka that Sonya wanted Saivon to create some sort of gris-gris to counter-act with the spell filled thunderstorm battering the city. The voodoo scientist locked herself away from everyone, aggravated that the infamous Voodoo Queen was incapable of creating the dark magic she was requesting. Saivon knew whatever magic she produced would be credited to Sonya and not her.


Dèsirèe sat at her table preparing herself for her next client's reading and tattoo. She didn't know much about the customer, only that they wanted her services and they traveled from out of town to meet with her. Bian walked in first through the beaded curtain that separated Dèsirèe's room from the front of the shop,

"Your 12 o'clock is here and he came baring gifts."

The cheerful co-worker handed the tattoo artist a handful of Mardi Gras beads and a very decorative Zulu coconut. Right then, Dèsirèe knew the person had to be from the city or knew the culture really well. She was admiring the detail in the coconut when a familiar voice bellowed in the room and a gentle smile came over the voodoo fortune teller. There stood the Voodoo Priest Baaloo with more gifts for her in his arms and Dèsirèe bypassed all of them as she wrapped the priest in a warm embrace,

"I can't believe you're here. How did you find me?"

"Word of a very powerful and kind Voodoo Queen travels fast."

"Baaloo, I'm no Queen. Just doing my part for the people."

"And that's what makes you a Queen. You are a servant for the people, and they aren't servants to you."

"Have you been able to talk to my grandpaw? How is he? I wanted to call but…"

"Robert-Earl was a very strong man; I will say that. I tried to pull him away from the danger, but New Orleans was also all he knew so he refused."

"Was? Why are you talking about him in past tense? Is he safe? Baaloo, is he safe?!"

The sadness on Baaloo's face told Dèsirèe all she needed to hear but she held onto one gleam of hope. She told the Priest she couldn't see her grandfather's spirit and those who have passed on she was always able to contact them on the other side. That's when Baaloo added to the horrid story about Dèsirèe's grandfather Robert-Earl. The Voodoo Mambo's stomach turned in knots from the pain of her loss and the next words that came from Baaloo just added to that pain. He told her how her granddad died from respiratory failure at a neighborhood hospice and that his soul was trapped in an amulet around Sonya's neck. The evil Voodoo Witch wanted to torment Dèsirèe into returning back to New Orleans so that she could finish what she started. Sonya knew if she had something Dèsirèe really wanted, there was nothing to stop her from coming back to get it. Baaloo begged for Dèsirèe to reconsider but he knew how she felt about her grandfather. He could see revenge raging in Dèsirèe's eyes as he attempted to calm the beast that was boiling to the surface. Bian overheard the entire conversation and stepped in,

"I call you my sister, not because we share the same blood, because we don't but because we share the same values. Know this, when you set out on a revenge-filled rage. Make sure you dig two graves."

"Bian, you don't understand. That's my family, literally the last of my family and she's holding him hostage like he's some kind of trinket around her neck."

"Family is everything. Trust me when I tell you I know what you mean but this is bigger than just us. I'm willing to help you with whatever decision you make but we need to be smart with this."

"I'm gonna wring her fucking neck."

Baaloo sat down with the girls, informing them of all he knew about Sonya and all the people that followed her. Dèsirèe couldn't believe how quickly the New Orleans Voodoo Queen acquired so much power in such a short period of time. She listened as the Voodoo Priest went down a list of officials and dignitaries that were at Sonya's every beckoned call. From law enforcement to political leaders, the Paris girl had them all under her thumb and growing daily. The small glimmer of hope was the urban legend that haunted the swamps of the Atchafalaya

River and the similarities of Sonya's baby sister. Baaloo stated he never ventured out to the swamp in fear of what he heard hunters say about the witch on the shoreline. Descriptions of the woman lead him to believe it truly was Trinity, but tales of a woman surrounded by wildlife, defending the area with pure wrath kept him away. The stories mirrored the Voodoo Priestess Julia Brown from Ruddock, Louisiana but with a much darker side because Trinity didn't allow anyone to roam her grounds. Dèsirèe knew she needed to get to Trinity and with her help take back New Orleans from Sonya's grasp.


Deep in the makeshift basement area of Maison Blanche, Saivon locked herself away from everybody. She was busy in her own feelings but creating masterful potions of voodoo at the request of Sonya. The rain that came down the day before had finally ceased but the flood waters were just receding early that morning. It wasn't a hurricane that came through the city, but the devastation left behind was too familiar to the residents of New Orleans. While the entire city attempted to clean up the mess from what was now called the '95 May Flood, Saivon paced in her basement. The rectangle-shaped windows that use to let light shine through were covered in branches and leaves that fell from the oak trees on the estate. Saivon could only see shadows of people walking past picking up debris outside.

Still angered from the audacity of Sonya getting
her to do all the work but never receiving any
kind of the credit. Saivon tossed around items
when she heard a knock at the door,

"Get the fuck from my door, I'm busy!"

"Cuz, it's me. You good?"

Hearing Douglas's voice calmed her a little as
she opened the door to him smiling with a bowl
of green grapes,

"Figured you needed a snack. You been down
here for hours."

"My bad cuz. Just down here doing master's
bidding I guess."

"Master, really?"

"That's what she act like. Like we her slaves or
something."

Douglas plopped himself up on Saivon's table
and reached out the bowl of grapes as a gesture
of understanding. She just leaned against her
cousin as she picked a few grapes from the vine
and continued to vent to him. Saivon felt
Douglas was the only one she could confide in
without judgement. She expressed how much she
was done with Sonya and how she wanted to just
leave what she called a cult. That the self-
proclaimed Voodoo Queen was a mockery of the
religion they followed, and that Baka was even
worse. Douglas just smiled as he nodded to
Saivon's angered rant but encouraged his cousin

to continue what he called the good work. Saivon then made a statement that changed the whole conversation,

> "I'm a see how great of a Queen she really is when she get a whiff of this poison I been grinding up. Let's see how strong she is then, play me like I'm some fool."

Saivon shared with her cousin the sabotage she had planned when she pulled out a small cloth bag from her pocket. The gris-gris was the total opposite of what Sonya asked her to create and Douglas insisted that his cousin reconsider her actions. Saivon walked away hell bent on destroying the Queen as she went to look out one of the windows that had just got cleared and let the sunlight shine on her face. When her eyes gained focus from the bright light, she could see her blood-cousin Douglas standing outside talking to the groundskeeper. Saivon knew right then she was in the wrong place at the wrong time and turned around with a sharp blade in hand. A quick grasp around her neck from the strong hands of Baka followed as skin that resembled Douglas peeled away from his face. His evil grin piercing through the falling flesh was the last thing Saivon saw. He slapped the knife from her hand and a puff of white powder sprayed in her face, knocking her out,

> "Stupid child."

Baka threw Saivon's limp body over his shoulder with ease and walked out the basement with her. He brought the unconscious Saivon to his Queen who sent him to investigate the potioneer's actions because she was suspicious of her. Sonya didn't trust anyone in her group and Saivon added to that distrust.


      Trinity sat quietly in her cottage meditating like she did every morning. It was her sense of complete peace before starting her day. It wasn't like she had a job to go to or a person to take care of, but Trinity kept busy. Tending to the swamp where she lived and the numerous animals in the area had its challenges, but she was content with her living arrangements. A true city girl turned Creole Cajun had its perks though and hidden away in plain sight was a plus. Trinity still held onto the idea of eliminating her sister but the thought of killing a family member was a huge factor that she didn't want to haunt her. The haunting didn't stop though because various visits from several **Loa** in the realm became more frequent after her summoning of spirits for the May Flood. The strong evoking of power that day caught the attention of **Loa** all over, some with good-spirited appreciation and others with nothing but evil intent. Trinity fought with temptation after temptation of Spirits promising powers and riches if she serves them. Angered **Loa** like **Marinette-Bwa-Chech**, a female she-devil would frequently visit, engulfed in flames and viciously slap Trinity in the face,

"Wake up bitch! You are no one without me."

"*Marinette*, not today!"

"I am every day, and these woods are mine. I only allow you to live here."

"*Loco* gave me this, not you, so leave."

Trinity knew the *Loa Marinette* didn't want any dealings with the more powerful Spirit *Loco* who had domain over the swamp. Her battles were mostly mental because the Voodoo Herbalist had to think fast on her feet when speaking with the *Loa*. Other *Loa* like *Ti-Jean-Petro*, a dwarf in stature with one foot but violent at his first appearance would try to trick Trinity in honoring him. *Ti-Jean* would roam through the brush in the swamp, leaving treats for the Herbalist to find. Knowing she would bless the food before taking it in *Ti-Jean* would wait for her response, but Trinity was too smart for him. Most of the time she would throw the offering in a flame or submerge it in the river,

"Not today little Prince. Maybe next time."

*Ti-Jean-Petro* was known to aid in black magic sorcery and knowing that her sister was deep in the art of black magic, Trinity didn't want any parts of it. Just like her violent visits from evil *Loa*, the loner also received visits from caring *Loa* like *Erzulie*, the goddess of love. *Erzulie* would try to touch Trinity's sensitive side and attempt to open her up to forgiving. Trinity would try to forgive but all the wrong

doings she's witnessed would boil up an anger
deep in her,

"Beautiful *Erzulie*, I can't forgive right now."

"You must try my child."

"Once it's done, I will."

"Waiting too long may make it too late."

"An arrival may open your eyes that you are not
the only target in this battle. Evil tries to insnare
us all."

Trinity didn't know what new arrival the spirit
was talking about because most of the residents
stayed clear of her in fear of becoming prey to
the swamps. She stayed to herself that day,
reflecting on good days in the watery forest but
chirps from nearby birds alarmed her that
someone was close. Trinity focused on a
shadowy image stumbling through the woods
towards her. She could tell just by how the
animals were reacting to the person, that it
wasn't humanlike by far. Alligators snarled, wild
hogs darted away, and water moccasins sat
upright as they hissed at the shadow figure.
Trinity prepared herself for yet another battle and
called on the swamps to give her strength. The
person came closer, gurgling sounds like
someone breathing under water began to
resonate through the brush and the horrid image
became clear. The afternoon sun shined down on
the undead naked body of a disemboweled
Saivon walking towards Trinity. Sadness came

over her as she stared into the sunken lifeless eyes of a woman, she used to consider a friend. Thoughts of Eli ran through her mind and sympathy began to overcome Trinity but then Saivon lunged towards her in full attack mode. The Herbalist called onto her strengths as thick green vines sprung from the earth, wrapping Saivon up and restraining the zombie where she stood. Trinity carefully walked up to the undead victim and noticed a note tied to her neck,

"I exert pure judgement on all those that defy me. I don't want this to be your fate little sister. Join me."

Trinity laid her hand on Saivon's forehead and began to say a blessing for her but then visions invaded her mind. She could see Baka throwing the woman on a sacrificial table, covered in all sorts of black magic symbols. Flashes of Baka ripping Saivon's clothes from her body like she was a ragdoll, and he was a sadistic rapist tormenting Trinity to no end. Images of Sonya completely nude dressed in only an open red silk robe holding a sharp curved dagger in her hand. Trinity couldn't turn away as she watched Baka hold Saivon's wrist over her head and Sonya slide the blade deep into her victim's stomach, filleting her open like a fish. Sonya pulled out Saivon's insides as the woman screamed out her last hurling cry. She could see Douglas close by with his pouch of undead powder and watched as he blew a handful of dust into the deceased victim's face, waking her from the dead. Trinity snatched her hand from Saivon's forehead and couldn't believe Douglas would do such a thing to his own flesh. She then realized the zombie maker had no choice or he faced the same. An evil laughter echoed through the trees as red eyes could be traced out, staring at the two standing in the middle of the clearing of the swamps. Trinity knew the laugh too well,

"***Kalfu***! You know you are not welcome here, be gone."

"Looks like my presence is needed here often. Nothing but dead come to you."

"Leave me demon and tell your servant her fate will end like this poor soul."

Right then Trinity commanded a pointed vine from the ground and like a cottonmouth rattler it struck its target with precision, piercing through Saivon's skull ending her pain. The Voodoo Herbalist stared back into the woods as the red eyes disappeared in disappointment. The war between the sisters gained another collateral damage in the form of another lost soul. Trinity made a place for Saivon's body right next to where she buried Eli.

## Chapter

Taking the first step back home was terrifying for Dèsirèe but it was something she knew she had to do. She had a strong backbone in her two companions Bian and Baaloo who both pushed for her to face her fears. It was easier said than done because they didn't have to face the woman Dèsirèe looked at as a sister for years. Knowing she had to kill her or at least that's what was going through her mind. Baaloo's stories of what was going on in New Orleans under Sonya's control were straight out of a storybook of some powerful witch using the people like puppets. Dèsirèe knew the Voodoo Queen had to be stopped and hoped she could reach Trinity before Sonya, because she desperately needed her help. The New Orleans Voodoo Priest convinced his counterparts to make one more stop before stepping foot in the city first. Their flight from Benin stopped in Haiti where Baaloo felt Dèsirèe needed to be, and her presence had mixed emotions. Like in West Africa, the religion was deeply rooted in the Caribbean, but some were strongly connected to the cursing of the religion as well as the blessings. Where in West Africa the religion was worn like an honor, Haiti wore it like armor. A warrior-like aura surrounded several residents of Haiti, from the flea market salesman to the military soldier. Some harnessed the aura as confidence as they went on with their day, but others used it as a striking force of intimidation. The visitors learned the history of the Caribbean country and how it fought for its freedom from slavery over a century ago. In 1803 rebels fought and defeated French troops that had control of Haiti. Voodoo was one major factor in the fall of the French as residents called on *Ogoun*, the *Loa* of war. *Ogoun* gave the people the strength, courage, and fortitude to conquer any enemy in front of them. Almost 200 years later, the warrior *Loa* roars through the streets of Haiti like a wild rhino and Dèsirèe could feel his spirit everywhere. Other *Loa* made their existence known also, in the eyes of passersby, windows of buildings, and even in whispers in the wind. Dèsirèe felt more surrounded by Spirits in the Caribbean Isle than anywhere else. She stopped for a moment to meditate and encircled herself in a barrier spell because she didn't want to be overwhelmed to the point where she couldn't focus. Once all the noise calmed in Dèsirèe's head she opened her eyes to a familiar face. The young woman she met from the market in Benin, when she first arrived, stood right in front of her. The *Loa* of the marketplace, *Ayizan* smiled as she held out her hand,

"I must say my child, you truly are a very powerful mambo. Come this way."

"How are you here?"

"Child, I am a God. I am everywhere."

Dèsirèe followed as *Ayizan* led her through the streets of Haiti to a small Voodoo Temple off the main roads. Even Baaloo didn't know of the place and just followed his friend. Dèsirèe's two companions didn't see *Ayizan* walking with her because the *Loa* didn't want to reveal herself to them. The doors of the temple opened to a congregation of followers of the religion and without hesitation welcomed the trio in. Just as *Ayizan* appeared she vanished into a mist before Dèsirèe's eyes, and the visitors found some seats. The temple service continued and Baaloo couldn't help but to ask his friend how she found the place. When Dèsirèe told him who brought them there he just smiled,

"Yeah, this is exactly where we supposed to be. You need this. I need this."


Trinity was done with hiding from her big sister. Life in the swamps had its pros and cons, its ups and downs but what pushed her to make the voyage back was the horrid memories. The Voodoo Herbalist saw with her own eyes the evil her own bloodline produced and enough was enough. Visions of what Sonya had done to people Trinity found herself connected to was the driving force that she had to be stopped. She knew the journey wasn't going to be easy, but it needed to be done. Trinity held a wrath deep inside that she was ready to unleash on any and every one that stood in her way. She just didn't know the battle was about to start as soon as she walked out the front door of her hideaway cottage in the swamps. The sun had gone down, and the moon rose as the only light that could be noticed for miles. Crickets, toads and all sorts of critters in the swamps announced themselves to the night as their adoptive mother prepared to leave. Trinity stepped out on the porch with only a backpack on her shoulder and a tote bag in her hand when she detected an unwanted visitor standing at the shoreline of the Atchafalaya. The she-devil **_Loa Marinette-Bwa-Chech_** looked out at the river as it flowed in her blood-red dress.

As she turned to walk towards Trinity, every footstep was fiery flames as the earth sizzled under her feet. The angered *Loa* spoke with a fierce agitation in her tone,

"You walking to your death, and I will feast on your rotting bones."

"I am not for your shit *Marinette*. Your servant will be the one under my feet when this is done."

"Either way, I will dine on a Paris soul soon bitch."

The night sky rumbled with thunder, sounds of iron chains breaking in the distance and a shadowy figure began walking towards the two women from the tree line. The squeal of a wild hog as it was dying echoed out, followed by its fat being chewed and devoured. Trinity could see it was a very large man, a large man with three horns perched on top of his head and eyes of fire. *Bosou Koblamin* was a *Loa* of violence, and his presence was one to be feared but Trinity stood her ground as he walked up to her. The massive *Loa* held the remaining parts of the wild hog in his hand, a bloody hind leg and bit off a hunk of flesh. *Bosou* stood there looking over the mortal standing in front of him as he chewed the meat of the pig and smiled. The three horned *Loa* looked over at the she-devil and his intense stare backed her down but not without her voicing out,

"You can't protect her all the time *Bosou*. Both of you will slip up and I will be right there."

"Be gone woman. Be gone."

**Bosou** commended Trinity for standing strong to **Marinette** and assured her that her travels would be watched over by him. The night traveler listened as **Bosou** told her he will be there for her when she goes to war with Sonya because he enjoys a battle. Trinity didn't know what to think of the mountain of a **Loa**, but she accepted his gift of cover as she made her way back to New Orleans. Leaving the swamp was a somber moment for Trinity and its occupants but she left the deep dense watery forest behind as she made her way to the low-lit freeway. She could see saddened glowing green eyes from the animals of the swamp watching her walk away, the tree line was covered with them. A large gray wolf appeared from the trees and began walking along side of Trinity as she tracked towards her destination. The Herbalist knew the animal didn't exist in Louisiana or even South America and once it made eye contact with her, she knew it was **Bosou**. He kept his promise to her and covering her every step to what could turn out to be a bloody family feud.


Service ended at the Voodoo Temple and the congregation emptied out onto the streets as smiles covered all their faces while they associated with one another. Baaloo found himself deep in discussion with the local Voodoo Priest while Bian talked with a few of the elders of the community. Dèsirèe casually walked through the small crowd of people just admiring the sights and enjoying the unity she felt with everyone there. The auras around the patrons of the Temple were bright pleasant colors that gave Dèsirèe a chance to let down her guard and relax. The pleasantries continued, even after seeing a woman sitting alone on a bench at the front entrance of the Voodoo Temple. It wasn't that the woman was doing anything out the way, she smiled at people as they walked pass and she really looked as if she was enjoying the collection of believers there. The thing that caught Dèsirèe's attention was that the woman didn't carry any sort of aura around her, not a glow or a shadow. It was something that Dèsirèe was able to see in anyone she encountered and the power she possessed gave her the advantage of how she interacts with them but not this woman. It intrigued her to the point where she couldn't take her eyes off of her not until the woman noticed her staring. Dèsirèe quickly turned to avoid eye contact but a whisper passed by her ear,

"It's ok my child."

As she peeked back, the woman gestured for Dèsirèe to come join her on the long wooden chair. It was as if Dèsirèe knew the lady at the Temple entrance was the one that whispered in her ear. Curiosity took over and Dèsirèe couldn't help but to see what the woman wanted with her. Before she could even greet her, the sweet scent of floral perfume met her first and then a smile.

The woman wore a silk black dress covered in red and blue roses all over, but her smile was what brightened anyone's spirit. Dèsirèe sat down on the bench with the woman, greeting her with a nod and a smile of her own,

"Hi, I'm Dèsirèe Glapion…"

"From New Orleans and those two with you are your friends, the Papaloi Baaloo and the very entertaining Asian girl Bian. Yes, my child I know exactly who you are."

"How do you know me?"

"Your powers supersede you my child. You are well known in my world. Your world just needs to catch up."

"No one else can see you can they?"

"They can see me when I allow them to. ***Erzulie Dantòr***, pleasure to meet you."

The woman on the bench released a smile as her image seemed to just blow away in the wind. Dèsirèe sat there in awe that yet another Spirit spoke to her again, giving her nothing but praise. Her highly energetic friend Bian came sat next to her with interesting news she received from the elder women she was talking to. A group of people were hiking to an amazing waterfall, Saut d'Eau, in the morning for meditation and enlightenment. Bian looked like a child in a candy store because of the stories she heard about the place. A 100-foot waterfall surrounded by a beautiful forest that could open your mind along with your heart and take away your burdens. The Haitian people said that the area and waterfall were blessed by the Love *Loa Erzulie Dantòr*. When Dèsirèe heard the name, she knew it was the place she needed to be and when Baaloo walked up he spoke about the sacred waterfall. The trio all prepared for their track in the early morn as they indulged themselves in the festivities the locals put together. Drums rang out to a melodic tone as patrons danced in the courtyard around brightly multicolored alters for various *Loa* of the realm. Dèsirèe watched as followers of the religion were taken over by Spirits during rituals and their mannerisms changed to the *Loa* that possessed them. Most of the possessions weren't violent but welcoming and after the *Loa* would leave them the people would rejoice in the experience. Drumbeats continued throughout as people from all over came together and embraced the religion of Voodoo. Bian watched as Voodooists danced in flames without being burned and was told by one of the practitioners that the feat is only possible because of the power of the *Loa*,

"See, in your faith you speak about God, but we become God, eh."

The Vietnamese woman didn't feel like an outsider or a visitor because just like in Africa the people of Haiti seemed to just take her in as one of their own. To the New Orleans natives, the scene was reminiscing of the Congo Square

Rhythms Festivals back home. Baaloo gazed in amazement as the people danced, chanted, and cheered to the beats of the drums. A unity, a collection and a oneness were felt all around them during the magnificent festival. Dèsirèe was a part of a collaboration of mortals and immortals all in one spot and at times couldn't tell the difference between the two. She was wrapped in wonder and did nothing but look forward to the morning travel to the mystical waterfall the residents spoke of.

Back in the city of New Orleans the Voodoo Queen Paris was preparing for yet another festive night with the dignitaries and criminal minds of the city. She pleasured in mixing the company of her visitors because she enjoyed the fortunes from both worlds. The powers and strengths from the politicians along with the everyday hoodlums were a combination Sonya used all to her benefit. The political backings she received in the city gave her full range to conduct any kind of business she wished. Properties became available that were otherwise off limits to everyday people, rules put in place that helped her succeed and government protection. The criminal side gave her an unlimited source of narcotics, henchmen, and street cred bigger than Capone himself. Some of the political figures still didn't buy into the Oracle's spiritual promises right along with some of the street hustlers. They were usually cast aside and left to fend for themselves in the monopoly Sonya created with her power groups,

"They will all end up following me because they won't survive without me."

For the most part everybody seemed to bow down to the Queen, including the reluctant Douglas who was still dealing with seeing how his cousin was treated. Standing there helpless as Sonya disemboweled her while she was still alive in front of him for disobeying her was pure torture. Being instructed like he was some sort of servant to turn her into one of his cursed souls was an agony that bubbled in his gut. He wanted revenge for Saivon's death but knew he would end up in the same manner if Sonya had one inclination that he went against anything she desired. Sonya wasn't foolish and had her faithful servant Baka follow Douglas's every move, but the shapeshifter was still a novice to the craft that Douglas perfected. With Saivon gone, Sonya relied on the dead woman's cousin to procreate the potions and gris-gris used during the rituals held at Maison Blanche. Douglas wasn't a specialist like Saivon, at making the powerful spell potions, but he put together a concoction of poisonous herbs unknown to Baka. Sonya's unwavering servant thought it was a collection of hallucinating herbs for the party, but Douglas knew it could be his freedom or his death. He just needed a way to have it passed to everyone in the main hall without the Voodoo Queen knowing.

Trinity's nightly travels became beneficial to her as her ghostly gray wolf companion and protector was always in close around. The *Loa* of Violence, **Bosou**, kept his promise and stayed by her side even though he had a reputation for not always being there for his faithful when needed. It was as if **Bosou** was making it his mission to watch over the Voodoo Herbalist. The Louisiana roadways tracked through dense forest along with immense swamp land and Trinity would always find a giving spot to relax during the day. Her days were protected by her old friend the *Loa* of vegetation and guardian of sanctuaries *Loco*. The powerful *Loa Loco* made sure Trinity was safe and secure during the daytime while **Bosou** took care of her at night. Her travels weren't without its trials as violent spirits and demons followed her too, trying to keep her away from reaching her destination. The Dark Spirit *Kalfu* would send out his demons to distract and terrorize Trinity while she made her way back to New Orleans. Demonic yellow eyes scurried in the shadows between the trees as they followed her, whispering threats,

"Die bitch. Die."

Growls and grunts could be heard through the leaves, but none were more threatening than the Black Magic *Loa Ti-Jean-Petro*. *Ti-Jean* went by many names, such as Prince Zandor or Congo Zandor but one thing was certain with the one foot having dwarf, he was the essence of evil. He was mean, spiteful, forever angered and a protector of sorcerers of black magic. Prince Zandor regarded Sonya as a powerful black magic sorceress and keeping Trinity away from her was his desired goal. The dwarf *Loa* would possess neighboring residents as Trinity made her way through their town with taunts, insults and splatters of spit to the face. She once stopped in one small Creole town to stock up on some supplies at a corner store when a cashier swung a knife at her,

"Fucking bitch!"

"What the fuck!"

"Your travels are useless. If you value the little life you have left, go back to your little hut by the river."

"You can't stop me, nor will you scare me. I will…"

"You will die bitch. That's what will happen, and my red wife *Marinette* will feast on your soul."

Trinity noted the mannerisms of the clerk as they hopped around on one foot and knew it was the dwarf *Loa Ti-Jean-Petro* taking control. She didn't want to hurt the cashier because she knew they had no idea to what was going on. Trinity avoided the swings of the blade as Prince Zandor advanced towards her but knew if the attacks continued, she would eventually get hit. The Herbalist called on her holistic strengths as strong vines sprung from the floorboards of the old corner store, wrapping the cashier up in a tight coil. The **Loa** Prince Zandor let out a frustrated yell as he left the cashier's body and Trinity walked out the store. She could hear the confused clerk calling for help as she made her way down the trail back to the freeway. Trinity knew she had to get out of town quickly because most mortals wouldn't understand what was going on or even try to.

**14<sup>th</sup>**

## <u>Chapter</u>

The early morning sun pierced through the window curtain as Dèsirèe gathered a few things from her hotel room. She and her friends were heading out to the sacred waterfall the town's folk spoke of the day before. Baaloo was excited to go witness the wonder the Haitian Voodoo Priest told him about and Bian was ready to bathe in the springs. Dèsirèe wasn't skeptical but she had her reservations about the place. She knew just like the well-wished manner people of the island knew of the waterfall, the ill-mannered and spiteful knew of it too. Dèsirèe was in search of nothing but good vibes on her journey to Saut d'Eau as she tried to clear her mind of any ill thoughts. She felt if she went to the waterfall with nothing but good intentions, good intentions would follow her there. After a short bus ride to the edge of the forest, the hike to the waterfall was marked out with a trail that was peppered with candles left behind by worshipers at the bottom of tree trunks. The crew observed offerings left behind also for the numerous *Loa* of the religion, good and evil. The sight unnerved Dèsirèe a bit and an old Haitian woman noticed the young woman's concern,

"You ok child?"

"I'm good. Just wondering, if this is such sacred grounds why would someone place an offering for the dark side and not the light?"

"Child, you believe in the Devil right?"

"Yeah, I guess so. Yes. From what I witness, yes."

"You do know the Devil was an Angel before he was cast out? Everything is poison, yet nothing is poison. Use something in a positive way and it will heal you. Use it in a negative way and it will kill you."

"So, it's a balance."

"Child you must understand the balance."

They arrived at the waterfall and the energy felt there was intense to the point where the entire area was electric. The closer the group got to the springs the more goosebumps rolled up Dèsirèe's back as her eyes just gazed at the beautiful sight. The lush green tropical forest was only the backdrop to a 100-foot waterfall that crashed down on algae covered large rocks at its base. The scene could only be described as complete beauty with its luscious greenery outlining a massive pristine waterway but at the same time a powerful waterfall. Chants, cheers, singing and drums bellowed through the forest as people camped out around the waterfall. The old Haitian woman pointed out to Dèsirèe the joy across everyone's face as they worshipped and cleansed themselves in the water. After listening to the wisdom, the elderly woman had to share with her, Dèsirèe watched believers walk up to the falls and bathe in its waters. Just like the elder told her, people let go of clothing as they washed in the waters, praying to the ***Loa Erzulie*** to bless them and wash away everything negative. The thing that caught Dèsirèe's attention was that with the large group of half-dressed or completely nude Voodoo patrons at the falls, not one person looked at the situation as being sexual. The human body was just that, a body and no one was there for primitive pleasures. Bian darted pass her friend as she handed Dèsirèe the tank top she was wearing and followed Baaloo up to the waterfall. Baaloo along with the Haitian Voodoo Priest helped the young ambitious Asian woman up the large boulders as the waters from Saut d'Eau splashed against them. Dèsirèe could barely see her friend between the showers but she knew she was safe with Baaloo close by her side. She giggled a little when the green shorts Bian had on, floated by in the stream and she knew her friend went all in with the ritual. Dèsirèe started to make her way up to the waterfall as she smiled at her friends walking down. She could see joy and content on Bian's face as she climbed down off the boulder she was standing on. Dèsirèe stood under the waterfall and the sound of the rushing waters drowned out everything around her. The pressure from the falls seemed to push every bit of stress right out and the New Orleans native let out a sigh of relief. She closed her eyes as the waterfall slammed against her body and without overthinking it Dèsirèe began removing her clothes. She threw her top down the stream along with the jeans she had on and began to meditate in the waters as she closed her eyes. Dèsirèe could feel a presence around her and assumed it was another worshipper joining her under the falls but when she opened her eyes no one was there. A whisper surrounded her, but the low hiss didn't sound anywhere friendly and more like an angered soul. Dèsirèe felt something was wrong and began to walk out of the falls but then the dark *Loa* of death **Baron Samedi** appeared in front of her. **Baron Samedi** snatched her by the throat and slammed her against the rock wall behind the waterfall. Dèsirèe attempted to get away from the angry *Loa* but his grip tightened the more she struggled. His long blood-colored wretched tongue slid from his mouth, and he licked the side of her face as he smiled,

"Oh that is sweet like honey. I will enjoy this."

"Release me demon."

"You are not in the position to make any demands girl. I will devour you where you stand. Your bones will become part of my collection of poor souls that attempted to go against me."

"Only if I allow it and you will not take me with you anywhere. Release me now!"

"Look at you. Nothing! Worthless! A waste of flesh. I will delight in destroying you."

*Baron Samedi* wrapped both of his hands around Dèsirèe's neck and raised her off her feet as he squeezed tighter. The daylight started to fade, consciousness was slipping between her fingers and the dark *Loa* looked as if he was winning this battle. Dèsirèe pulled and kicked at the *Loa* of Death as he tried to choke her out. Then the air became thick with the scent of perfume as the woman from the Voodoo Temple appeared behind him. Still dressed in her black silk dress covered in the red and blue roses, the woman placed her hand on *Baron Samedi*'s shoulder and he fell powerless to her. *Samedi* released Dèsirèe and in return was raised off his feet by the woman as she grabbed him by the throat,

"Now you know this is my sacred grounds demon. No one and I mean no one touches my followers unless I say so."

"*Erzulie*, you can't protect her all the time!"

"Don't show your face here again *Samedi*."

The same way **Baron Samedi** appeared, he was gone in a dark mist and *Erzulie* helped Dèsirèe to her feet. She had no words for what she just witnessed but was grateful to the beautiful **Loa** standing in front of her. *Erzulie* wrapped her arms around the young soulful spirit and whispered to her that everything would be okay if she believed in herself. A calm like no other came over Dèsirèe and she began to release all the stress she ever felt in tears as they rolled down her cheek. She closed her eyes as whispers of affirmations spewed from *Erzulie*'s lips to her ears and then the **Loa** of Love was gone. Dèsirèe stepped through the waterfall to a new day in her eyes, her friends Baaloo and Bian could see the change in her. She was ready, with her sights on reclaiming her homeland back from Sonya Paris.

Maison Blanche was beaming with so much energy that it glowed in the dark night sky. Sonya sashayed through the hallways of the mansion, in her red see-through silk dress, making sure every detail she wanted for the big party was carried out to perfection. The Voodoo Oracle was talking with one of her many maids when she noticed a barefoot guy in a straw hat leaning against the wall. The dark-skinned young man didn't look familiar but when he made eye contact with Sonya, he smiled at her as if he knew her. She wasn't in the mood for any games as she stepped to the young man,

"The party ain't starting for another hour and you most definitely not dressed for the occasion. Can I help you with anything?"

"Oh child, I'm here to help you."

"Me? And how may I ask can you help me? Do you see where you're standing? All of this is mine. I don't think you can help me in any way."

"You town folk are so oblivious, you can't see the dagger coming at you because of all the glitter in your eyes. Complete idiots. Living off the backs of the hardworking man yet taking all the credit."

"Enough with the riddles. Who are you and what is this help you speak of?"

"Me? I'm **Zaka** but a lot of people call me cousin, cause I'm friendly like that. You and my brother are real close, **Baron Samedi**. Yes child, you can close your mouth now or I might find something to shove in it."

"**Zaka**? Why are you here? Shouldn't you be out with the lower class, giving them hope?"

"Oh, so you do know of me. Your rival Dèsirèe is a lot more inviting to my presence. Guess it's the high and mighty city folk attitude in you."

"Enough Spirit, what is it?"

Sonya knew of the *Loa* of agriculture, farmer by trade and little brother to the Spirit of Death **Baron Samedi**. She knew he was just as lude as his big brother but lacked in sophistication like the Baron though. Sonya also knew the dark *Loa* was infamous for gossip and was always ready to tell it all to anyone who was willing to listen to him. *Zaka*'s eyes lit up with fierce flames of excitement while his evil grin outlined the jagged teeth in his mouth. He had Sonya's full attention when he told her of secrets, he held on his lips about her entire group. Secrets of how some of her maids pocketed money given out at her party functions, how her guards would make sacrifices for themselves and not for her liked they all promised. *Zaka* laughed when he told the elder of the Paris girls about her loyal servant Baka's naked rituals, he performed in private in honor of her while touching himself constantly. The biggest secret the gossiping *Loa* shared with Sonya was that of Douglas's plans of poisoning her entire party. The enraged Voodoo Queen began to storm off to find the undead reanimator and deal with him, but *Zaka* whispered suggestions of torture in front of everyone. *Zaka*'s reasoning was to scare any and every one from thinking of crossing her again. Sonya listened to the dark *Loa* as he caressed her body for his own pleasures and hashed out a plan of her own to put Douglas on display for everyone to see. She left *Zaka* leaning against the wall with his devilish grin, as she made her way to the courtyard where some of her guards were. When the Queen turned back to get another look at the *Loa* of gossip, he was gone leaving nothing but white smoke in his absence. Her mind raced with all sorts of torture she had planned for Douglas, but she needed to find where he was hiding first.


Trinity made her way through the wooded areas of Destrehan, Louisiana and tracked through the city of Metairie. The city of New Orleans was finally in sight, and nothing was stopping her from getting to her destination. The aura of her sister's powers grew stronger the closer she got to the city and the Herbalist found a nice spot on the outskirts of City Park in a large oak tree to rest her bones. The *Loa Bosou* kept his promise to the end as a large gray wolf guarded the base of the tree while Trinity slept peacefully during the night. She made sure to get some rest because the morning would bring on a battle, she wasn't ready for with her own flesh and blood. Trinity prayed for the weakness for her sister to leave her because she knew Sonya would use it against her. She knew that the self-proclaimed Voodoo Queen would stop at nothing to destroy the one thing standing in her way. Whispers rustled through the leaves of the oak trees like affirmations,

"She is not worthy of the title and strength is not your only ally. Light will shine again."

Trinity felt somewhat relieved because she knew she had the Spirit of Light on her side and that she wasn't alone in this fight. She didn't want to end Sonya's life, but she knew if it came to a decision, she would choose life. As her eyes became heavy, Trinity gazed at the night sky and the bluish-black sky was clearer than ever. Stars glistened, the moon was a full bright white and the creatures of the night all announced themselves with their unique sounds. Crickets chirped, frogs croaked, one night owl occasionally hooted and it all was like a bedtime song to Trinity but then it all stopped suddenly, which caught her attention. As she peeked between the trees an ominous tall muscular figure walked towards her and growls from the alert gray wolf at the base of the tree rumbled through the leaves. The closer the dark figure got to where Trinity was the louder the wolf snarled until it darted towards the shadowed silhouette. Once the beast was in reach, it lunged at its victim but was swatted away as if it were an annoying fly at a picnic. Trinity's eyes widened at the sight of her protector being manhandled like a toy and the mighty wolf whimpered off into the brush as the large man came into view. The dark image was the *Loa* of Black Magic, *Kalfu* and he smiled with a sinister grin as he looked up at Trinity perched in the large oak tree,

"Tell me that wasn't your only source of protection child."

"*Kalfu*, you're not wanted here!"

"Oh, no one ever wants me to be anywhere, but I come anyways because I can."

"Be gone demon! My quarrel is not with you but your servant."

"If your issues are with one of my followers than your quarrels are definitely with me child."

The dark *Loa* grew in size and began to reach out to his victim in the tree but then Trinity heard the loud breaking of chains, announcing *Bosou***'s** arrival. The large three-horned giant rushed through the brush, with war in his eyes and knocked *Kalfu* off his feet onto his back. The *Loa* of Violence stood over a stunned *Kalfu* and demanded him to leave his faithful follower alone. The arrogant *Kalfu* rose to his feet, dusted the dirt from his black suit and walked up to *Bosou* without a care in the world. *Bosou*'s chest swelled as he stared down his enemy,

"Are you sure you want these troubles? We can fight for all eternity, and I still won't allow you to get near her."

"You fool! You are gonna stand between me and a simple mortal?"

"Yes! Now like she said, be gone demon."

Knowing he couldn't beat *Bosou* even if he tried his best, *Kalfu* disappeared from the wooded area and the sounds of the night returned with his absence. Trinity climbed down from the tree to thank the mighty *Loa* who sat back down at the base of the large oak and found herself resting in his lap, wrapped in his massive arms. She was finally able to close her eyes and get some much-needed sleep. Trinity knew morning would come soon and the fate of her or her sister would result in one of them not seeing the next morning.

Luxury cars lined the driveway of Maison Blanche as high-class figures along with high-paid street pharmacists made their way in. It was a mixed crowd inside, but they all were there to celebrate their Queen of Voodoo. Sonya's manipulation of the religion for profit and power gained her the following she desired from day one. Politicians worshipped her, drug dealers respected her, and the underbelly of the city all honored her as their Queen. The crowd grew as the patrons filled the courtyard and Sonya sat under a wide magnolia tree that had a semi-circle wooden bench at its base. She watched as her loyal followers marched in with gifts for her and she just nodded at them with approval. Sonya's mind was occupied with the betrayal she had learned of and finding Douglas was all she wanted. Her wishes were granted when two of her guards walked through a cluster of people, escorting a battered Douglas. With Baka seated on her right and Senator Patterson along with Mayor Morales on her left the guards brought Douglas in front of the lady of the house. One of the guards pushed on their prisoner's shoulder to bow before their Queen but Douglas stood strong refusing to budge. A hard kick in the back of his thighs dropped him to his knees in front of Sonya and she smiled,

"Now why you being so mean Dougie? You know it's always my way."

"Fuck you Sonya!"

"Now Dougie…"

"Stop calling me that shit bitch!"

One of the guards punched Douglas in the side of his head for disrespecting Sonya in front of him and the victim fell to the ground at her feet. He lay there knowing his suffering wasn't going to be quick because a swift death was never Sonya's style. All the party-goers knew Douglas was part of Sonya's crew and seeing him like that had them all confused. The hostess began to announce to everyone the plans the captured had in store for them all and rumbles of anger waved over all those in attendance. The crowd turned into an angry mob in need of blood and Sonya was ready to give them exactly what they wanted. She stood over Douglas, grabbed a handful of his shirt collar and dragged him through the courtyard to a wooden pole that was set up just for the occasion. The old wooden pole had some antique iron shackles, that were more than likely used during slavery times, fastened to the top of it and leather straps at the base. Sonya had her goons put the restraints on Douglas and the crowd cheered as they spat along with throwing drinks in his face. At that point

Douglas knew he was all on his own and didn't care what anyone thought of him,

"You fucking idiots following behind a she devil that can care less if you live or die! She passes out trinkets and tell you it will bring you power, and riches and you fill her pockets with all your prized possessions. She hasn't done anything for any of you and you still follow her! Fuck your Queen! Fuck all of you! Fucking clowns!"

Baka had enough of Douglas's rant as he slapped him across the face, drawing blood from his lip. He then handed Sonya her favorite curved dagger and she smiled with sights on slicing through her victim's flesh. Douglas knew his end was near and began to pray out loud for mercy but then a dark shadow rose from behind the pole he was strapped to. Demonic blistered hands pierced through the dark shadow, covering his mouth and pulling his head back exposing his neck to Sonya's dagger. The *Loa* of Death *Kalfu* then came from behind the pole, accompanied by the evil-spirited *Loa Marinette-Bwa-Chech* who announced herself to everyone,

"Bow your heads, you wretched mortals or I will feast on your bones! Witness the true Red Queen and She-Devil of them all. I am *Marinette*!"

The crowd couldn't believe what they were seeing as the evil spirited *Loa* walked around and every footstep produced flames as they touched the ground. *Kalfu* made his way to Sonya, whispering in her ear that he just left from where Trinity was and that they will more than likely see each other soon. Sonya wanted to confront her sister right then, but the powerful *Loa Kalfu* advised against it because he knew of the protection Trinity had at the moment. The Voodoo Queen gained everyone's attention from the boisterous *Loa Marinette* as she got back to the handcuffed Douglas,

"Don't think we forgot about you Dougie. *Marinette* will definitely eat good tonight. You know she likes fat pigs like you."

"Fuck you Sonya."

"No Dougie, fuck you."

Sonya stood nose to nose with Douglas as she looked in his eyes and slowly pushed the curved blade into his stomach. Douglas refused to give her the pleasure of screaming or showing any pain as his assaulter turned the dagger in his gut. The pain was excruciating, his body shivered, and his blood spilled out onto the dirt under his feet. After gouging open Douglas's abdomen, Sonya began to pull out his insides, all the while still looking deep into his eyes waiting on that moment of death. Blood gurgled up his throat and he started to choke on his own fluids. Sonya reached up in his ribcage, grasping hold of Douglas's spastic beating heart and pulled it from his chest and showed her followers. She held it up high so everyone could see, while staring Douglas in his fading eyes as death took over and uttered,

"No one will cross me again. You was the last of them. *Kalfu*, his soul is yours to do as you please."

The *Loa* of Death reached in the body of Douglas pulling out a screaming ghostly image of the tied-up dead man on the pole. Douglas's soul fought to get away from *Kalfu*'s deadly grasp, but it was all for nothing as they all disappeared into the dark shadow with all the demonic hands. The message was sent that anyone that thought of betraying the Voodoo Queen would face the same fate.

# Chapter

Her travels through Haiti had opened Dèsirèe to so much that her belief in the religion that sent her life into a tailspin began to look very promising. As she looked out the window of the plane flying over the Gulf of Mexico, she started to see some familiar landscape she hadn't gazed on in a very long time and a little bit of nervousness seeped in. Bian could see the wave of emotions running across her best friend's face and knew it had to be terrifying coming back to the place where so many people wanted her dead. Baaloo on the other hand was war-ready, with confidence that Dèsirèe was more than capable of dethroning Sonya and taking over the title of New Orleans's Voodoo Queen. He also was prepared to face his twin Baka in an attempt to direct him to the light or send him to the spirit world. Dèsirèe appreciated the support from both of her friends and drew off their energy as a driving force. She watched from her window seat as the plane sliced through a cluster of snow-white clouds and the massive Mississippi River came into view. It was as if the aircraft was following the large waterway as it curved through Louisiana's terrain. The plane began to slowly drop down and Dèsirèe clinched the armrest of the seat she was in, flustered at what's to come next. Bian tried her best to ease her worries the only way she knew how,

"We going eat as soon as we touch down right? And I ain't talking bout no tourist food from some high-priced restaurant. I need that authentic New Orleans soul food."

"I gotchu."

"Now I do wanna stop and get some big nets from that place in the French Quarters."

"Big nets? What is a big net?"

"You know what I'm talking bout. Big nets. From that place Café Du Monde."

"Girl! That's beignets! Oh Lawd, she called dem big nets. I needed that laugh."

The plane had finally touched down and the stewardess started to instruct everyone to their exits. Baaloo led the way as he grabbed his bag and the two besties followed right behind him as they laughed over Bian's butchering of a French word. The aircraft finally stopped on the tarmac of the Louis Armstrong New Orleans International Airport and the stewardess opened the exit door as the airstairs came out for everyone to leave. Dèsirèe stepped out and the first thing to hit her was Louisiana's thick humidity. It was a feeling she didn't know she missed so much, a thickness in the air that filled her lungs and made her smile that she was home. Dèsirèe walked down the stairs just taking in the feeling of being back home, being back to where it all started for her and how it all came full circle with all her travels. She made one step on her homeland, the clouds rumbled with thunder and a spiritual wave roared through the city, as if to announce her arrival. It was an energy that just shock waved out from under her feet and the entire Voodoo realm knew Dèsirèe had arrived. She walked towards the Terminal where a taxi was waiting for them all but before getting there Dèsirèe recognized some familiar faces. With her own special abilities still intact, Bian nudged her bestie with a big smile on her face when she noticed them too. Standing at the end of the walkway was Lucas with Marie Laveau's daughters, Felicite and Angelie, but another person was with them. Joy came over Dèsirèe seeing her friend again but the closer she got to him the other person began to look more and more familiar to her. The light-skinned woman who haunted her dreams for years was standing right there with the three spirits that guided her to her truths. Dèsirèe didn't know how to take it but once Marie Laveau smiled at her, she knew her presence was everything. Lucas and the daughters stayed silent as Laveau walked up to her,

"Child, we been waiting for this moment. You have finally arrived, and you will right so much wrong in this city."

"Do you believe I can, because I'm not sure."

"My child, you must believe in yourself first. Spirit can only help if you believe you can, and I know you can."

"Thank you Queen."

"Find your friend Trinity, she needs you. You
need each other."

Dèsirèe didn't know Trinity was still alive and to
hear Laveau call out her name added to the
pleasantries in her heart. She told her company
what Laveau said, and they knew they had to
find the Herbalist to complete them.


Sonya was stretched out in her king-sized
bed enjoying some vigorous head game from her
loyal servant Baka. The couple wasn't alone as
Senator Elizabeth Patterson found herself under
the covers with the Voodoo Queen and the
shapeshifter. Baka indulged himself in satisfying
both women as his tongue twirled around
Sonya's delectable clit and he slid two fingers
deep inside the Senator's warmness. Their
bodies intertwined all around one another
generating a hot box as sweat dripped from their
bodies. The trio fondled each other erotically as
Baka took turns pushing himself deep inside the
exotic women in front of him. Sonya enjoyed
watching Baka ravage Patterson's tight pleasure
pocket with his hardened manhood while the
Senator pleased her with her tongue. The
pleasures were reaching their peak as Baka had a
tight grip of the politician's hips, shoving every
inch of himself in her lushness. Patterson also
had Sonya in a euphoric state as she sucked on
her throbbing clit bringing her to the brink of

exploding in her mouth. The walls of the bedroom were sweating from the body heat in there and ménage à trois was on the verge of releasing their orgasmic juices, but a jolt ceased everything. It was as if an electric field rushed through the house and it was a powerful presence for Sonya, so much that it shook her and not in a good way. The Voodoo dark magic Queen sat up in bed and was looking around as if someone walked in the room,

"What the fuck was that?"

Baka and the Senator both were caught off guard, thinking they did something wrong when Sonya stopped their session without completing it. Senator Patterson timidly began gathering her clothes, avoiding eye contact with the Queen as Baka stood at the end of the bed asking his master how he could help. Sonya walked around the room looking out every window for the source of the blast of energy she felt. Sitting in a lounge chair off in the corner of the room, in the shadows, puffing on a cigar was the ominous *Loa Kalfu*. Sonya's master looked beyond pissed as smoke expelled from his nostrils,

"Get rid of them peasants. We need to talk."

Sonya ordered her loyal followers to leave her and as soon as they left, still as naked as she was born, crawled to *Kalfu's* feet. She kneeled at his side as he placed his hand on her head and told her she has trouble coming her way. Sonya was oblivious to the arrival of Dèsirèe and *Kalfu* was angered at the landing of the one person he knew could dethrone his appointed Queen of Voodoo. She listened with the attention of a model student in a classroom as the enraged *Loa of Death* spoke,

"Your mortal mind was busy trying to lure your feeble little sister to your side and your nemesis was busy gaining strength."

"I'm so sorry. I thought she was dead by now."

"Did you see her dead corpse? No, you didn't. You assumed and you know what happens to those that assume."

"I beat her once; I can beat her again. She's afraid of me."

"You better hope she's afraid of you because she's not the same frail soul you remember."

"I promise, her soul will be under your feet."

"If it's not I know of a soul my loins will be pleased with."

"Tell me and I will get them for you."

"You simple mortals truly don't understand. Eyes closed with open palms, only to find me reaching out to them. The soul I'm talking about is yours, fool. Defeat Dèsirèe or dwell in the pits I prepared for you."

"Master wait!"

*Kalfu* disappeared into dust from the chair he was sitting in, leaving Sonya on her knees still begging for him to come back. She knew she had to find Dèsirèe and Trinity before either of them got to her. The Voodoo Queen called for Baka and the devoted minion rushed through the door as soon as he heard her. Baka informed her that he had Senator Patterson's driver bring her home and that he had all the guards secure Maison Blanche. Sonya got on the phone to call the Senator about her secret mercenaries and told Baka to get in touch with all the street goons he could find. Sonya was prepping for war and was determined not to lose grip of the reign of power she possessed.


The city of New Orleans looked the same way it did when she ran away from it all and Trinity proudly walked the streets without a worry in her spirit. She felt the radiant energy from a history long before her and soaked it all in like a sponge. People walking pass her were a little guarded because the barefoot backpack wearing hermit-looking young woman seemed out of place. Everyone pretty much assumed she was a homeless woman just walking through looking for a handout. Trinity paid them no mind as she just took in the sights of her city. She made her way down Basin Street towards Louis Armstrong Park where the historic Congo Square resides. The square held so much history for the black community, some history few knew of and was the breeding ground for so much of the life of the Voodoo religion in New Orleans. Trinity knew she needed to touch that area, soak in its energy, and meditate before thinking about approaching her sister. She made it to Congo Square and to an outsider it seemed like a normal park with plaques peppered all-around of historical events. Trinity relished in the life of the park, images of its history, celebrations of the past and ghostly figures that walked about its grounds. She sat in the grass, listening to Spirits speak to her with positive affirmations, giving her strength to face all her fears and doubts. A young man dressed in a Louis Vuitton jogging suit and a thick gold chain with a gold diamond clustered number 9 medallion walked up to her meditating,

"You look real familiar."

"I truly don't believe you know who I am."

"I do believe I do, Trinity. Yo sister got a lot of her people looking for you."

"Are you one of her people?"

"Nah. My mama believe heavy in that Hoodoo stuff but I don't trust that witch Sonya."

"Smart man. And what is your name? I mean it's only right you tell me; you already know mine."

"Neville. Neville Wilson. Look, you might wanna stay lowkey out here. A lot of these goons not as nice as me. Be safe Trinity."

"Be blessed Neville Wilson, yes be blessed."

The young man left to meet up with a few of his friends walking around in the park. Trinity kept an eye on him as he walked away and noticed that the company he was with noticed her. She could tell just by the reaction on their faces that they knew who she was, and Trinity took Neville's advice. She gathered her things and made her way out of Congo Square but not until she came across a very powerful *Loa* that roamed those grounds. *Papa Legba* walked up to Trinity, without saying one word gave her his blessings and grace then vanished in front of her eyes. She felt the *Loa's* presence surrounding her like a blanket but knew she needed to move around. As she passed the group of men Neville was with, she could hear the conflicting conversation between them,

"Dawg, that's her!"

"Nah, we not steppin' to her."

"Nev, yo moms gone be mad we let this bitch make it. The Voodoo chick got paper on her head."

"She is not to be touched by us. Are we clear? I'll deal with my mama."

*Papa Legba's* covering was like a protection, along with the kindness she saw in the street thug Neville. His gentle eyes glanced over at her, and it was as if he was watching over her every move out of the park. Trinity went on her way and just like Neville told his crew she was untouched by any of his men as she walked by them. She was in a good place mentally, the Spirits continued to speak to her, and the Voodoo Herbalist walked to her destination. Facing her sister Sonya was no longer a fear in her head and Trinity had one more stop to make before heading to Maison Blanche.


The taxi pulled up in front of Baaloo's Voodoo Temple and the crew carried their bags inside. The Voodoo Priest was relieved to be back home and to have his companions with him was an added satisfaction. He escorted Bian to the back of the Temple to show her the sleeping quarters while Dèsirèe stayed up front by Baaloo's podium. The newly returned native found herself instantly meditating as soon as she sat down, and a calm came over her as she pulled in the energy from all over. It was as if Dèsirèe was having an outer body experience because she could see herself, everything around her plus everything around the Temple. The visions brought her outside, moving through the city streets, through neighborhoods, above trees, and even darting between buildings. It was like her soul was searching for someone and Dèsirèe just went with the flow until she realized who the search was for. Her heart raced, her body began to sweat, and her muscles tightened when she noticed every woman that popped in her visions resembled Trinity in some way. Dèsirèe's subconscious was literally combing the city for her friend. Young black girls and women flashed into view at a rapid pace until a young woman walking barefoot on The Riverwalk came into view. The young woman's aura radiated wholesomeness, love, honor but it also moved with rage attached to it. Once she caught sight of those hazel green eyes, Dèsirèe knew she had found her friend and she simply smiled in her spirit. She could tell the Trinity she remembered and the one she was seeing now were two totally different people. The sweet quiet girl walked with determination, bothered no one but took no shit and demanded respect. Dèsirèe's spirit reached out to Trinity,

"I've missed you so much."

"What the hell."

"Come to Baaloo's Temple, we'll be waiting for you."

Dèsirèe came out of her trance, body still tingling from the experience and faint whispers still ringing in her ear. She ran to tell Baaloo the news of finding Trinity, but darkness hovered over her. Some of the whispers Dèsirèe heard earlier became stronger, louder and a little threatening. She started to hear the talking surround the Temple and the conversation didn't sound appealing at all. Dèsirèe went to the sleeping quarters where Baaloo and Bian were chilling, but dialog of military action on the Voodoo Temple followed her like a duckling would its mother. The conversations became clear when she caught glimpses of men holding assault rifles with silencers on them, running on the Temple grounds in her mind's eye. Dèsirèe knew they weren't there to pray and she knew Baaloo wasn't one to fight gunfire with gunfire, so she summoned the next best thing. Bian had been there to witness her bestie talk or call on *Loa* of the realm before, but Baaloo never had the opportunity. He watched the calm Glapion girl's eyes roll white, speak a language of the ancestors and electricity filled the room. The men Dèsirèe visualized surrounding the Temple were inches from entering the holy place when the sound of chains dragging the floor and an owl hooting echoed through the building. A rumble ran through the walls of the Temple, like as if a giant was stomping down the halls and the floorboards shivered from front to back. Dèsirèe's eyes locked in on the front door and she shouted,

"Protect this house and protect us! Do as you will!"

Fog filled up the Temple from the floors and two massive figures stood up from the mist, ready for battle. One was the three horned *Loa* that watched over the Herbalist on her journey back to the city and the other was a massive muscular black in color protectorate by nature *Loa* who demands respect. ***Bosou,*** the ***Loa of Violence*** stood next to ***Brise***, the ***Loa of the Hills***, and they both rushed the front entrance of the Temple as soon as the mercenaries kicked the door in. The mortal men didn't have a chance against the powerful *Loa* charging them as their guns went off in every direction, bullets ricocheting off the walls and the floors. Bodies flew about, slamming against the walls, bones breaking were only muffled out by the screams of the men in agony and laughter from the two giant Spirits followed. Baaloo wouldn't have believed it if he hadn't seen it with his own eyes but still, he was bewildered at the display of power. Bian stood there watching as her friend conducted a strategic attack on all those that came to bring harm to anyone in the Temple. Dèsirèe's companions watched as *Brise* and *Bosou* finished off the last of their prey, tossing the bodies in an abyss of darkness like trash, discarded forever. The dynamic duo stood proud of their works as they looked to Dèsirèe for confirmation. She nodded her head and the two massive *Loa* disappeared along with the mist they arrived in. Baaloo stood frozen, not of fear but just being mystified from the feat he just witnessed. Bian stood still too because she knew her friend needed a moment to decompress from such a tall order she commanded, but she was still concerned for her,

"Dee! You good?"

"I'm alright. I'm alright. Anybody hurt? Y'all ok?"

"Girl we good."

Once Bian saw that Dèsirèe was talking she knew she could approach her and just wrapped her arms around her. The Glapion girl just collapsed in her friend's arms and Bian happily held her up. Baaloo started picking up furniture, putting things back in place and looking over bullet holes in the walls he needed to repair. He didn't know what to say to Dèsirèe, but he most definitely wasn't afraid of her because he knew her heart and he knew she stood for what was right. The trio got together and began to clean up the Temple when they heard a knock at the busted front door. Dèsirèe looked up to a smiling Trinity who broke the silence between them first,

"Y'all threw a party and didn't even invite a muthafucka."

16<sup>th</sup>

---

## Chapter

After some deep cleaning, a lot of sweeping, a little carpentry, and a bunch of jokes from Bian, the group all sat down for dinner. They talked while they were cleaning up, but no one really got into any details on what life was like outside of New Orleans. Trinity was a little guarded because her time from her hometown was traumatic and she was still feeling out everyone around her. She listened as Bian talked about meeting Dèsirèe for the first time and being able to see her three spiritual companions. Trinity was intrigued at Bian's ability,

"So you're able to see Spirits?"

"Yeah. Been able to see them for as long as I can remember. My parents thought I was just making up imaginary friends when I was little but as I got older, they thought something was wrong with me. Like I was possessed or something."

"Very few understand the Spiritual World. They assume it's something completely separate from ours but it's actually part of us, intertwined and woven into the fabric of our lives. Its special people like you that are capable to see both."

"Yeah, like those two young men that been following you ever since you walked in here."

Trinity looked over her shoulder to see nothing there and asked Bian to describe the men she was referring to. Tears began to fill her and Dèsirèe's eyes when the young Asian woman gave descriptions of Micah standing alongside of Eli. Baaloo attempted to hold his composure, but his feelings took over and he wept also over the young men he knew for a short period of time.

The clairvoyant addition to the group didn't
know exactly how much she helped Trinity to
heal in that moment. She knew all about Lucas,
heard stories from Dèsirèe about Eli and Micah
but she didn't know the gravity of their presence
with Trinity at that moment. After hearing Bian
describe two people that meant a lot to her,
Trinity really went into detail on where and how
she survived. She told them how Douglas
brought a horde of zombies to her front door
with a zombified Micah leading the way. They
all listened as her voice trembled when she told
them how Eli was murdered right in front of her.
The group was shocked to hear Saivon had fell
victim to Sonya's tyranny and became a zombie
like messenger. Trinity let it all out and just
letting the words spill from her lips was like a
release of burdens. Dèsirèe couldn't believe all
the things her friend went through, and it angered
her so much that it all was because of one
person. The one person they both thought cared
so much for them and Baaloo could see the rage
building,

"Sister never go into a battle with revenge in
your heart."

"I know, I know cause if I base it all on revenge I
might as well dig two graves. I heard it before,
no need to preach to me about it."

"No, I wasn't gonna preach. Revenge clouds
your judgement, and you need a clear mind to
fight this one. Sonya and her Dark Spirits will
use that against you. Trust me, I lost my twin to

the Darkness, and I know the pain that goes with that."

The group knew they had to think hard on how they were going to approach Sonya's mansion because they knew the Voodoo Witch was going to be heavily guarded. Trinity told them about the young man she encountered and the message of the bounty on their heads. Looking around his Temple and the destruction that was left behind, Baaloo knew it was all facts.

No one was ever allowed on the third floor where Sonya's meditation room was, even Baka couldn't go up there. Not that she never brought anyone up there with her because she has, they just never came back down. Rumors spread like wildfire between her staff that Sonya wasn't only the Voodoo Queen of New Orleans but a vicious cannibal too. Simply because they would never see the body of the one, she escorted upstairs ever again. Sonya never corrected them and allowed the whispers to be an added reason why no one was granted access to the third floor. Two armed guards were always on the second floor, posted at the stairs that lead up to Sonya's sacred area. The only way she could be contacted was through an intercom but everyone in Maison Blanche knew not to disturb her once she was up there. The last person who made that fatal mistake, undead corpse is still roaming the swamps in Tangipahoa and their beating heart sits in a glass case on the mantle as decoration.

Sonya made sure all her staff knew the rules of her house and always reiterated the third-floor rule every time she walked pass the guards,

"Anybody that tries to get by you needs to die on these steps and if they do pass you, you will die on these steps."

Rumbles, mumbles and all sorts of sounds could be heard from up there, but no one ever knew what exactly went on up there or what the third floor looked like. Sonya would lock the large engraved wooden double doors at the top of the steps, get down on both knees in front of a large altar covered in lit candles and assorted sacrificial bones to pray. A green mist would spew from behind the altar, filling the room with a haze and groans of anger rattled the walls of the room. Sonya's eyes fell to the floor like an obedient servant and *Kalfu* walked through the fog,

"What do you want peasant?"

"Only to serve you, my lord."

"I see you haven't corrected your Dèsirèe issue yet."

"I promise, I'm working on it my lord."

"You're not working hard enough!"

*Kalfu* snatched Sonya by the neck, lifting her off the floor and she dangled like a ragdoll in his hand. The greenish fog changed to deep red, and the she-devil *Marinette-Bwa-Chech* entered the room, placing her hand on *Kalfu's* shoulder. The angered *Loa* lowered Sonya back to her feet as his interest turned to the seductive evil spirit who suggested allowing her to help. *Marinette* wanted to assist in getting rid of their servant's adversaries and called on a fierce *Petro Loa* like herself to join her sadistic fun. *Kongo Savanne* was a maneater and pleasured in grinding human bones for his meals. He was a very handsome, articulate and well-dressed deviled gentleman. *Kongo Savanne* walked through wearing a pure white suit with a white fedora and only his fiery eyes peeked from under the brim of his hat. *Kongo* released a grin as he looked over at *Kalfu*,

"Seems you have a pest that needs to be terminated. Allow me to feast on them."

"What do you want Kongo? Because I know this service not free."

"C'mon Kalfu, I'm doing this out the kindness of my heart."

"Demon, you don't have a heart."

"That is true. Just give me a few souls to chew on. I really like the virgins, their bones so sweet."

*Kalfu* gave the well-dressed *Loa* permission to hunt down Trinity and Dèsirèe, while he gave Sonya orders to gather her followers together. *Kalfu* was done waiting on Sonya to assert her wickedness through the city like she promised him. She begged her master for forgiveness, and he responded with a backhanded slap to her face. Sonya fell to the floor, on her knees in front of the one that reigned over her and all she could hear is laughter from the three *Loa* that stood over her. The angered dark Spirit repeated himself to her again about getting all of her followers together. The she-devil *Marinette-Bwa-Chech* wanted in on the fight because she wanted to tear Trinity apart ever since her first encounter with her at the Atchafalaya River. The Master of Evil gave the go-ahead but with conditions,

"Witch I need you to scare her. Make her believe she will be harmed but her blood shall not be spilled. One drop and you will have to deal with me."

"Whateva Kalfu, whateva. I'm here for blood. Remember, red is my color."

"Witch, you can have all the blood you want but hers."

*Marinette* disappeared in a burst of flames and the handsome gentleman known as *Kongo Savanne* vanished in the fading fog that filled the room. Sonya was left alone with the Dark Force of *Kalfu* hovering over her as disappointment filled his eyes of her. He stood her up from her knees, encouraging her to please him with the strength and power he bestowed onto her. Sonya continued to make promises that Dèsirèe and Trinity would bow down to him in the end. *Kalfu* in return made a promise of his own and Sonya knew if she didn't succeed, she would be tortured for all eternity. The Dark Spirit left her in the ritual room with all sorts of thoughts running through her head, but one thing continued to poke at her. Through everything she had acquired, everything she accomplished in that short period of time. Sonya started to realize, she made a deal with the Devil himself and her soul was on the chopping block.

Baaloo walked the French Quarters with Trinity while Dèsirèe and Bian stayed back at the Temple. They walked down the old brick roads of Decatur Street, pass the French Market and found themselves being tourist in their own hometown. The Voodoo Priest wanted some alone time with the Herbalist because they been apart from each other for so long. He knew where Dèsirèe's head was when it came to Sonya, but he had to truly feel Trinity out. The idea of being secluded in the swamps for months at a time with no one around could rattle anyone's mind and Trinity's sanity was a concern. Plus battling a sibling with a strong sense that only one of them would make it out alive was another worry. Baaloo needed to know if his young friend would choose them or her own flesh and blood when it came down to it. He didn't know what or how to ask and the Herbalist had a feeling something was bothering him. As they made their way through the antique

New Orleans' architecture, looking at buildings
that were over a century old Trinity spoke up,

"You good my friend?"

"Yeah. You good?"

"I'm good. Trust me, I'm good. There's no need
to worry bout me."

"Trinity, I'm not worried. I just…"

"Wondering if I'm some kind of nutcase, with
powers and might go crazy on everybody.
Houngan, I've been through a lot, but one thing
is for certain I'm standing ten toes down with
more sense around me than you may know."

"I believe you my sister, I believe you."

"Good, cause we need each other right now. As
long as I know y'all got my back I have yours."

Trinity's statement brought a smile to Baaloo's
face, and they continued their journey through
the Quarters. They found themselves standing in
front of the Voodoo Museum on Dumaine Street,
it was as if their souls were drawn to the place.
Baaloo opened the glass paned double doors to a
candle lit entrance way. Artifacts, paintings, and
voodoo paraphernalia were scattered all around
the room. Trinity hesitantly entered the building
because chills came over her as if something was
wrong with the place, but she trusted she would
be safe with Baaloo. She could hear rumbles and
moans through the walls of the museum but
when she looked over to her companion, he

seemed unbothered. Indescribable whispers of a woman's voice flew pass her ears making Trinity fidgety and slight touches on her skin were unwanted. It was as if she was surrounded by spirits but couldn't see not one of them. Baaloo started talking with the female caretaker of the museum and the two where in deep conversation about the place. Trinity's eyes darted back and forth looking around while the conversation Baaloo was having with the woman fell to mumbles in the background. It wasn't until she heard the woman mention standing in the swamps of the Atchafalaya that the Herbalist started to pay attention. Once Trinity looked in the woman's face, flashes of *Marinette's* fire filled image came out staring her down with evil intent. Baaloo had no clue of the danger he was standing in the middle of. He quickly found out when he flew across the room as the she-devil ***Marinette-Bwa-Chech*** revealed herself. All the doors of the museum slammed shut, locking them inside with the laughing Voodoo Witch,

"Looks like I finally have you to myself without your three horned guardian Bosou to back you up."

Trinity went to help a stunned Baaloo off the floor as *Marinette* levitated over them. The menacing she-devil began to cause all sorts of items to fly off the shelves, walls and nearby tables, circling her victims. Baaloo was still dazed as books along with voodoo artifacts slapped him and Trinity in the face. The Voodoo

Priest's friend had enough of the **_Loa's_** antics and began summoning powers of her own. Trinity's eyes rolled white as her arms outstretched calling on the Spirit of Vegetation to her aid and the floorboards of the museum began to rattle. Bright green vines sprung from the floor, breaking through concrete and wood with force. The vines wrapped around Baaloo, protecting him from **_Marinette's_** onslaught as Trinity covered him. Some of the vines became an extension of Trinity's arms as they snapped objects out the air and reaching out to the she-devil that was floating towards her victims. The **_Petro Loa Marinette_** lunged at Trinity, but the Herbalist's counterattack stopped the witch in her tracks. The evil spirit was restrained, with every limb stretched out and a thorn-filled vine wrapped around her neck. **_Marinette_** tried everything to break free from the animated vines but the more she struggled the tighter the grip Trinity applied until the angered **_Loa_** gave up. Baaloo looked up from the floor to see the devilish Spirit staring him down as Trinity held her captive in her grasp. **_Marinette_** shouted and cursed the Herbalist,

"Release me bitch!"

"Be gone from this place Marinette, you are not wanted here!"

"I come as I please mortal! I can feel you weakening, and I will come back stronger. Your bones will be my dessert."

"Leave us witch."

A burst of flames flashed, filling the room as *Marinette* disappeared and the vines Trinity controlled fell to the floor. Baaloo pulled himself together as his friend helped him to his feet, his eyes still stunned from what it just witnessed. In the 20 years the Voodoo Priest been studying the religion, he had never experienced anything like what he had just witnessed. The pure power Trinity expelled was amazing and scary at the same time, but Baaloo knew her heart, he knew she was part of the Light. The Light that would cast the Dark back into its abyss and save them. Trinity felt they needed to get back to the Temple because that assault seemed like the beginning of something much worse.

Drumbeats could be heard rumbling out the doors of the Voodoo Temple on Rampart Street and the city embraced the sounds. It had become a joyous gathering of like minds when people from different cultures, religions, and races found themselves drawn to the beats. It was as if the drums spoke to their souls and Dèsirèe along with her bestie Bian welcomed the cheerful company. People started to see the Temple as more of a community center than a religious building. Mardi Gras Indians found themselves dressing up and dancing to the drumbeats in front of the Temple. A collaboration of elaborate colors sprayed across the front of the Voodoo Temple as cheers and chants echoed out.

Catholic along with Baptist preachers found a common ground in their sermons and had an impromptu session on the sidewalk, in front of a mass of people. A multitude of races, Black, White, Asian along with many more all came together to rejoice and not one soul had an evil intent in their spirit. A light smiled deep inside Dèsirèe, seeing so many people get together in front of her. She admired so many auras of goodness glowing from everybody in attendance, she almost forgot about the evil undertones she was there for. It wasn't until she noticed a man weaving through the crowd, dressed in a pure white suit, that something didn't feel right. Dèsirèe could barely see his face under the white fedora he had on his head, but his eyes peered straight at her from under the brim. She saw fire when she looked at him, but his smile was in a word, gorgeous. Bian had the handsome guy in sight too and nudged her friend when she noticed the smile on both their faces when they looked at each other. Dèsirèe stayed shy, refusing to make the first move but her energetic counterpart not so much as she made her way towards the man in white. Bian stood in front of the man and reached out her hand,

"How you doing?"

"Aren't you just delicious. I could just eat you on a kabob."

"Now that's a good one. My name is Bian and that beautiful woman over there is…"

"Dèsirèe Glapion, I know."

"You know Dèsirèe?"

"Yes. Yes, I do. She is very well known around here."

"She is? Well, you know so much about her. She would love to get to know you."

"I'd like that."

Bian took the gentleman's hand as she escorted him through the crowd towards Dèsirèe. The closer they got to her the more nervous she became but then the nervousness went away when an old friend appeared in the crowd with worry on his face. A faint image of Lucas stood in front of her, shaking his head no as Bian walked up to her with the guy in white. Dèsirèe didn't know how to take the so-called warning but it all fell to the side when the gentleman walked up to her and took off his hat. He had that wavy Creole-Indian black hair, red-hazel-colored eyes, light caramel complexion, full lips and a smile that could melt ice. Dèsirèe was lost in his charisma as he held her hand but as soon as he greeted her, she knew everyone around her was in danger,

"Kongo Savanne, nice to finally meet you Dèsirèe Glapion."

"Why are you here demon?"

"Aww, c'mon now. Demon? Really? I'm no demon."

"You're a demon in my eyes."

"Before I gave you my name, your eyes only saw someone you wanted to fuck. Still wanna fuck? Cause I do."

"What do you want?"

"I just want to be friends, offer you a way out. But if you refuse me, I'll delight in eating you alive."

***Kongo Savanne*** disappeared right in front of both the women and then Lucas appeared in front of Dèsirèe screaming for her to run. In the far distance an invisible force appeared, it was like a raging bull running through the crowd, throwing people about heading straight towards Dèsirèe. She stood her ground as the crowd of people started to run away, yelling for help and Bian shouted for her friend to run too. The ominous force pushed people down at Dèsirèe's feet, but no one was standing there in front of her. She frantically looked around, searching for any sign of the violent ***Loa Kongo Savanne*** but he could not be found. The screams from Bian quickly alerted her to the front door of the Temple where she seen ***Kongo*** holding her friend off her feet by the neck. The mean Spirit looked Dèsirèe in the eyes and smiled as he dragged the terrified young woman in the Temple with him, slamming the doors shut behind him. Dèsirèe ran to rescue her friend as people outside picked themselves up off the ground, helping the wounded after ***Kongo's*** rage.

The inside of the Temple was dark and freezing cold but echoes of Bian screaming in pain brought on extreme fear in Dèsirèe. She searched for her friend to only find her nailed to the back wall of the Temple behind the pulpit where the devilish **Kongo Savanne** was standing. Tears rolled down Dèsirèe's cheek as she stared up at her friend impaled with rusty iron nails in her wrists and feet. **Kongo** slammed his hand on the pulpit to get her attention,

"Now, like I said before. I'm offering you a way out of all of this."

"Speak demon!"

"There you go with that demon shit again."

"Tell me what you want!"

"So feisty. I see you want to get down to business. Look, you take your little egg roll here and go back to wherever you came from and never return. Leave New Orleans, leave Baaloo, leave Trinity behind you and I won't have to feed on you."

"Release my friend."

"So, we have a deal?"

Dèsirèe wasn't giving into the vicious Spirit just yet and called on reinforcement as the **Loa Erzulie Dantòr** appeared in the Temple. The beautiful Spirit looked around at the destruction **Kongo Savanne** created and shook her head in disgust. Dèsirèe then shouted for the demon to release her friend from the wall and all she got in return was laughter. She could see the arrogance on **Kongo's** face as he charged towards her, shattering the wooden pulpit into splinters. Dèsirèe stumbled back in fear but the powerful hand of **Erzulie** stopped **Kongo** in his tracks,

"Now, now Kongo. You have done enough here. Every Voodoo Temple is my domain and you're overstepping your boundaries, time for you to go."

"Get your hands off me bitch!"

"Language young man. You don't want me to call my husband to deal with you, eh?"

"Bring the old fool! Nobody's scared of the has been warrior Ogoun, haven't been for centuries."

"I was trying to be nice, so be it."

**Erzulie** released the angered Spirit and rumbles of thunder rattled the building, then a lightning bolt flashed. The large warrior **Loa Ogoun** stood in front of them all, enraged and ready for battle as his eyes pierced into **Kongo Savanne**. Every step of the powerful Spirit was a loud thump to the building, shaking everything around him. The two **Loa** lunged at each other in a fierce battle and Dèsirèe scattered out the way. While the Spirits were engaged with each other, the frightened mortal ran to her friend who was still nailed to the wall. Dèsirèe pulled out the rusty nails and an unconscious Bian fell in her arms. Blood poured out of Bian's wounds and

Dèsirèe attempted to bandage them with torn cloths on the floor. Groans and growls filled the building as **Ogoun** and **Kongo Savanne** went to war with one another. The **Loa of War** overpowered **Kongo** and had him pinned against the wall. The battle was won by the warrior Spirit and **Kongo** was being dragged back to the Voodoo realm. Dèsirèe helped her friend Bian up but **Kongo** had one last trick,

"Not yet bitch!"

The evil Spirit threw an iron spear straight at Bian, sending it right through her back and coming out her chest. Dèsirèe's friend went limp and fell to the floor as she screamed at the sight. A glowing image of Bian's soul floated upward, and a heavenly light embraced her. Dèsirèe's screams filled the Temple,

"No! No! Bian, no! Not like this. Not like this."

Everything around her faded to black, the sounds of **Kongo's** laughter stabbed her soul and agony was the only thing she could feel. Dèsirèe didn't know what to do but faint sounds of Trinity and Baaloo calling her name pulled her out of her darkness. She looked towards the door of the Temple, through the blur of tears filling her eyes to see Baaloo and Trinity rushing to her side. She sat on her knees crying, holding Bian in her lap as her friends attempted to figure out what happened. Police and ambulance sirens could be heard approaching in the distance but

the only thing taunting Dèsirèe's spirit was the
faint sound of ***Kongo's*** laughter.



## Chapter

News of the failed attacks on Trinity and Dèsirèe angered Sonya to destroy her office while Baka along with Senator Patterson watched in fear. Chairs flew across the room, end tables smashed against the walls and a 100lb office desk flipped on its side. Not one inch of the Voodoo Queen's office lay untouched after her wrath was released on it. Senator Patterson attempted to offer her assistance, but Baka held her with a gesture of silence at the moment while Sonya calmed herself. Baka had witnessed his Queen's anger before and knew speaking would only fuel her to lash out. The Senator didn't know what to do but sit and watch as Sonya finally calmed down from her tantrum,

"Ms. Paris, you alright?"

"Yes, Elizabeth. I'm fine. Why are you still here?"

"I didn't want to leave you upset. You looked like you needed to talk to someone."

"Oh, you was my shoulder to cry on? I doubt that seriously."

"I'm just trying to help here."

"You know how you can help, bring me Dèsirèe, that dredlock-wearing Voodoo Priest Baaloo and my raggedy ass little sister and place them at my fucking feet! Can you do that?! Get the fuck out my face."

The Senator left Sonya in her office with Baka and ran into Councilman Trevor Jackson on her way out. The two politicians talked secretly in the driveway about how the Voodoo Queen was losing grasp of her following. They knew she still had a hold on the mayors and city officials that ran the police force. But some of the elite and powerful people of the city along with a few of the criminal elements stepped away from the Voodoo lifestyle Sonya hashed out. After the demise of Douglas at her last big party, many of Sonya's followers had enough of her tyranny. Councilman Jackson was one of those followers who was ready to walk away but was afraid of what Sonya would expose of him if he did,

"Do you understand how that would ruin me? How that would ruin my family?"

"Trust me, I definitely don't need my shit spilled out on the streets either."

"So, what do we do? We can't just tell her no."

"I know but we can't go down with this ship either cause it's sinking, and you know it."

"Talking like that, you wanna end up like that dude Douglas?"

"Do you? Exactly. So, keep quiet until I call on you."

The Senator left in her car while the Councilman went inside to drop off his weekly donations to the Voodoo Queen. Councilman Jackson made sure his drop-offs were always right on time, not because he was loyal but because he needed his little secret kept a secret.

The secret many of Councilman Jackson's voters
didn't know about him was that he was part of a
very powerful drug family. The criminal family
got caught up in Sonya's web and in order to
keep their lucrative operation going along with
keeping Trevor Jackson's seat on the board safe
they paid the Queen weekly. The Councilman
was fed up with the payments and Senator
Patterson's scheme to get out from under
Sonya's thumb looked very appealing.


        NOPD squad cars began making their exits
from in front of Baaloo's Spiritual Voodoo
Temple after an extensive investigation of what
happened in and outside of the voodoo chapel.
Bian's death was labeled a homicide during a
vandalism by an unknown suspect and Dèsirèe
was the only witness. A detective handed the
distraught friend his business card, letting her
know to call him if she remembers anything else
about the suspect that came in the Temple. A
slew of people was still recovering from the hit
and run that occurred outside in the street, while
medical teams assessed injuries. The sirens from
multiple ambulances could still be heard driving
down the street as the Voodoo Priest closed the
front doors to his place of worship. Trinity didn't
know what to say to Dèsirèe because she knew
the hurt she was going through. She had just met
the Asian firecracker and was feeling a pain deep
within herself. The building lay quiet while
Baaloo and Trinity tried cleaning up once again.

They didn't even bother looking for Dèsirèe to help but she stood herself up from the corner she was crotched down in and started putting things away. The Voodoo Priest just watched as she moved about but his mind was rambling with questions. He watched Trinity conjure up Spirits as if she was opening up a menu at a restaurant and attested to Dèsirèe doing the same. Baaloo needed to know what or who he was dealing with and had to know as he asked Dèsirèe,

"What really happened here?"

"What do you mean? I loss someone really close to me. That's what happened."

"Sister, I'm not trying to be inconsiderate. Please understand that. I'm just trying to understand all of this."

"My apologies. I'm still trying to process all of this and lashing out at you is something I don't want to do. You need to know, Bian was truly like my sister. No judgement, just love and understanding. And that demon stole that from me."

"I understand, I have grown to love her too. But I'm trying to process all of this too. In all the years I've been studying the religion I've never been around two individuals like you. I have watched people be taken over by Spirits but never use them the way you two have. How is that possible? Then you say all those people outside were thrown around by a Spirit they didn't see but then every witness out there say it was a drunk driver that ran through the crowd. I'm just trying to figure all of this out."

"It was a simple suggestion spell. I used it before but never that big. I didn't think it would work but it did."

Baaloo listened as Dèsirèe told him that she was able to control a person's mind if she needed to, that it was one of her gifts. She knew when the police arrived, they would start questioning people and everyone needed to be saying the same thing. So, she used the same powers she used on the racist Chalmette police officer she used a long time ago. Trinity remembered that terrifying night in Chalmette and how they discovered their powers were much stronger than they knew. The Voodoo Priest sat himself down as he listened to both the women in front of him talk about how they defended themselves, using the gifts they had. Baaloo adored the wonders in both of them but feared that they could waiver from the light,

"Be careful my sisters. Just like our dear Sonya, all the darkness need is a little to creep in and use you."

"Baaloo, I am nothing like her. She chose her path a long time ago. All I want to do is extinguish it now."


Hurricane season had started, and the city prepared for another year of storms, but Sonya had her own storm brewing deep inside her. The self-proclaimed Queen of the city saw her loyal followers dwindle down to under half from what she had at the beginning of the year. She knew she needed to do something drastic to gain their respect again, mere fear wasn't working in her favor. Thoughts of what she may do if disobeyed turned to what can she really do in a lot of people's heads. Sonya needed a strong display of her powers in front of a crowd. She called on one of her faithful followers Mayor Lacroix,

"My sweet Sebastian, I need you."

"I'm on my way Queen."

"No, stay there. I need you to get a message to your people on the docks. A storm is coming, and I want them to stay safe, get their boats to higher ground."

The request was somewhat strange for Mayor Lacroix because Sonya was never one to show concern for others, unless it was for her benefit. Even though the weatherman said nothing of any storms approaching, Sonya was adamant in telling the mayor his city would be hit hard by a storm of great magnitude. She stressed to the mayor that her visions showed her serious damage to the fishing docks in Chalmette. Sonya also told Lacroix that her visions showed her that her followers would be saved if they obeyed her wishes and find the two women responsible for the disappearance of their fallen officer. Through all the events that have been going on, the mysterious vanishing of Officer Milson fell to the wayside and Mayor Lacroix wanted the names of the women. Sonya knew at that moment she had the feeble-minded mayor where she wanted him,

"My dear Sebastian, the names will come in with the storm. As soon as I know, you will know. Me and Baka are on our way to you now, to prepare."

Sonya ended her call with the mayor and began to put more pieces together in the chess match she was arranging. She knew she needed opponents coming at Dèsirèe and Trinity from all angles in order to make them surrender to her. Sonya's rivals proved to be very formidable when hit head on, so she planned on an all-out attack. She called Mayor Morales next,

"Hello my sweet Morales, your services are needed."

"Whatever you need."

Sonya told the mayor she needed the two women that were questioned about the homicide at the Voodoo Temple to be detained at one of his precincts. Mayor Morales was a little confused to why because the investigation proved them to be innocent, but he made the call anyway. Just like with the mayor from Chalmette, Sonya told the city of New Orleans mayor she had visions about the incident that proved them to be guilty. With police cars in route to the Voodoo Temple, the Queen of

Voodoo plan was set in motion to destroy her enemies.


The spiritual building on Rampart Street finally started to look like it did when Dèsirèe first walked through its front doors. Everything was put back in place and a calm came over the three individuals that helped restore a sense of normalcy back to the Voodoo Temple. Dèsirèe was stacking a few of Baaloo's book collection back on the shelves when a chill came over her. It drew her attention to the front of the building and all of a sudden there was a knock at the door. Baaloo was in the back cooking and didn't hear the knocking, so Trinity went to see who it was. When she opened the door there stood Senator Elizabeth Patterson and Councilman Trevor Jackson. Neither of the politicians knew what Trinity, Dèsirèe or the Voodoo Priest looked like, but Senator Patterson needed to speak with them desperately. Trinity had an uneasy feeling about the visit,

"How can I help you? Better yet why are you here? Because your presence feels like I'm about to get an earful of bullshit."

"You must be Trinity. There's only one other person I know with that much fire on her tongue and that's your older sister."

"What do you want?"

"Straight to the point I see. Can we come in? This is real important, no games, no tricks."

Trinity stepped to the side to let the two strangers in, and Senator Patterson waived her security driver off. Once inside Dèsirèe noticed a glow of positive auras emitting from both of the visitors and she gestured for Trinity to relax a bit, just so they could hear them out. Councilman Jackson got right to business when he told them that they needed to pack up their belongings and leave the Temple. When asked why, he informed the group that Sonya had a SWAT team on the way with all intent to kill if they resisted. Senator Patterson confirmed what the councilman said and added that the mayor of New Orleans along with Chalmette were out for blood. Baaloo came from the kitchen in the back furious,

"You come here, calling yourself trying to save us from a slaughter but if I remember right, you two use to be right at Sonya's side when she would bark out orders. What happened, she cut you off and now you're bitter?"

"No. She didn't cut us off of anything. We just tired of the nonsense. She's doing too much, and she needs to be stopped and you two are the only ones we think can stop her."

"You gave the devil the keys to your city and now you want them back. You do know if she finds out you betrayed her, she'll be coming after you too."

"The whole reason we coming to you. Y'all need to stop her. We have a few people on our side that thinks the same way."

"Well, what we waiting on?"

Trinity grabbed her backpack and Dèsirèe along with Baaloo snatched up a few of their things as they all headed out the back of the Temple to avoid being seen. Senator Patterson's driver was waiting for them, and the entire group packed themselves into the all black Suburban. As the dark vehicle made its way to Esplanade Avenue, several vehicles began pulling up in front of Baaloo's Temple and a brigade of officers jumped out. The Voodoo Priest cringed when he watched them kick in his front door and at least 20 lawmen rushed in with 20 more surrounding the building, searching for anybody. Patterson told her driver to slowly go past the SWAT team's vehicles and got on the phone, telling whoever was on the other end that they were on the way. The voodoo trio crotched down in the Suburban as it drove by, police lights flickering in the night sky and their anxieties were on an all-time high. Trinity's psyche started to mess with her because seeing the vehicle they were riding in brought back some difficult memories. Thinking she was losing it; the Herbalist just shook it off believing that stress was just getting to her. She sat quiet in the backseat as the large vehicle raced down Rampart and every streetlight they went pass, shined inside. Every time light would brighten the inside of the dark Suburban, Trinity would get a glimpse of the stuff packed in the very back and her eyes got big when she started to recognize some things. Combat gear and automatic assault rifles showed her that her mind wasn't playing tricks on her. Anger filled her spirit as she shouted,

"It was you! Stop the fucking car!"

"What?"

"It was you the whole damn time! Stop this fucking car!"

"Trinity, what are you talking about."

"You muthafucka! If you don't pull the fuck over right now, you gone wish you did."

Luckily the driver had made it to their destination, parking in front of a blue two-story shotgun house on the corner of Burgundy and Lizardi Street. Across the street from the blue house was a bar room that was still buzzing with customers stumbling in and out of it. The doors to the Suburban swung open and everybody got out, with Trinity still upset with what she assumed about Senator Patterson. Dèsirèe tried her best to calm her friend down but when Trinity told her about the gear, she saw in the back of the SUV the tables were turned. Tears were streaming down the young Herbalist's face when she shouted that the Senator was the reason her friend was dead. Patterson attempted to explain but Trinity wasn't trying to hear any of it as her rage took over and the grass on the sidewalk began to grow at her command. Senator Patterson's driver witnessed those amazing powers firsthand and began to back away, but a long vine stopped his retreat, wrapping around his ankles, dropping him to the ground. Right when Trinity was about to unleash her wrath on the two politicians in front of her, three young men walked out of the blue house, where two of the men greeted them,

"Well, well, well, welcome to the lower 9th ward. The C.T.C., most people say it mean Cross the Canal but you in Cut Throat City baby."

"Man-man chill out. They know where they at, hey Trinity. Let's get y'all inside, looks like a storm coming."

Right when she stared into those gentle eyes of the street thug from Congo Square, a wave of calmness came over Trinity. There standing in front of her was Neville Wilson and the Herbalist knew she was safe with him. Neville escorted everybody upstairs into the blue shotgun house while the other two men that were with him stayed outside on the sidewalk like two watchdogs.


Neville was right about a storm coming their way. Sonya stood on a small bridge on Paris Road that was right next to Bayou Bienenue in Chalmette with her hands raised to the sky. Her chants called on the *Loas* of lightening, wind and

rain. The clouds overhead darkened and
rumbled; flashes of electricity surged across the
night sky. Standing behind Sonya were three
very powerful ***Loa, Sogbo, Bade and Mombu***
who were giving her all the strength she needed
to create the ultimate storm. The earth literally
shivered under her feet as the waters began to
splash back and forth in the Bayou. One large
lightning bolt crashed down from the clouds and
the sky opened up to a torrential downpour.
Sonya's vision was all coming true in the eyes of
the people of Chalmette. Waters from the rain
quickly overpowered the streets, flooding every
inch of the city and its residents were trapped.
Mayor Lacroix watched from his office window,
the powerful storm that raged through his city
and wondered if his plead for the shrimp boaters
to move to higher ground was heard. He could
see old oak trees give into the weight of the
storm and collapse under pressure. The tops of
buildings peeled away like wrapping paper and
sheets of siding flew through the air. The lights
in his office flickered every time the thunder
shook the building and as fast as the storm came,
it simply stopped. Mayor Lacroix's secretary
rushed in his office telling him to turn on the TV.
A drenched news reporter stood in knee high
water telling a story of the city's savior,

"If you look at the top of the convenience store,
  you can see the young woman still chanting to
  the sky. We've learned her name is Sonya Paris
  and she is the certified Voodoo Queen of New
  Orleans. Residents around here said that Ms.

Paris arrived right after the storm began and got
to the roof of Ladeaux's corner store, where
she's been the whole time. Chanting an ancient
Voodoo chant warding off the storm that ravaged
through our town."

The reporter went to a few people that were
still standing around and asked them what they
saw. Mayor Lacroix smiled as he listened to
people claiming that the woman on the roof
saved Chalmette from drowning. He joyed in the
idea that everyone declared his Queen as a
saving grace in what was such a horrid time.
Little did the unknowing admirer know was that
Sonya was the one that brought on the deadly
storm to his city. Mayor Lacroix continued to
watch the news report as people cheered for the
Voodoo Queen who came down from the roof.
The flood waters began to recede, the clouds
cleared from the sky and the stars along with a
full moon lit up the night air as people cheered
for their savior Sonya Paris the Queen of
Voodoo. Sonya's plan worked out perfectly and
she had an entire city backing her this time. The
self-proclaimed Queen made her way to Mayor
Lacroix, and he welcomed her with opened arms
as he embraced his dominatrix,

"You did it. You saved my little city. I thank
you."

"My sweet Sebastian, you meant to say my little
city. I didn't do this for nothing. Get on your
knees, I need gratification for my services."

Sonya raised her red skirt, revealing her freshly waxed pleasure point and the mayor did as he was told. He dropped to his knees in front of her, pleasing her with his mouth. Sonya had full control of the man in charge of Chalmette and all access to all of its attributes. With her leg still propped on the mayor's shoulder and he continued his due diligence in pleasing, Sonya produced a tattered sheet of paper that had two names written on it. She dropped the paper on his desk and told him those were the names he needed to seek vengeance for the missing Officer Milson. Mayor Lacroix noticed one of the names was Sonya's own sister and he asked her if she was sure she wanted him to search for her. The sinister Voodoo Queen just nodded her head yes as she walked out of the mayor's office to Baka waiting for her in a red Cadillac.

18<sup>th</sup>

## <u>Chapter</u>

Two weeks had gone by since Trinity arrived at Neville's safe house in the lower 9th ward. She along with Dèsirèe and Baaloo discovered a collection of people that wanted the Queen of Voodoo dethroned. Senator Patterson proved her loyalty to the trio by using her political powers to deter the police from coming around the hideout. Stating the neighborhood was going to police themselves in order for law enforcement to respond to more important task. The Senator even explained to Trinity how she was blinded with greed through Sonya's illusions and was embarrassed to disclose how she was drawn in. The trust between the two began to become stronger when Patterson told Trinity that her and her men were pawns used at Sonya's will. Councilman Jackson made sure Sonya's rivals stayed safe also with anonymous tips of sightings all the way across town. The Councilman's actions were out of fear of being caught, not by Sonya but his drug family being caught by the feds and going to jail. Councilman Trevor Jackson's whole purpose was to keep the group safe until they were ready to make a move on the Voodoo witch, he feared possessing his secrets. The haven on Burgundy Street became a home away from home for the three refugees. The fridge stayed stocked with food and at least two guards stayed in the downstairs apartment to make sure no one bothered them. Dèsirèe started to lose the will to ignore the music blaring from the bar across the street from them. The Mercede's Bar always had something going on every night and the Mardi Gras music coming out the front door was like a lure to her. One night she couldn't take it anymore and ventured out on the front porch which only made it worse, so she made her way down the stairs. Before she knew it, Dèsirèe was standing at the corner looking through the front door of the bar and one of the guards stopped her,

"Girl, wha cha doing? Y'all suppose to stay inside."

"I just have to see what's going on. The music just calling me like a serenade."

"Girl dat damn Voodoo Witch gone be the only one calling yo name if you don't get yo ass inside."

"Sonya don't scare me. Not anymore."

"I've been there to see people go in Maison Blanche and not come out."

"Well, I'm bout to go in this bar and the only way I'm coming out is with a buzz."

Dèsirèe stepped off the street corner and before she could take another step, Trinity grabbed hold of her hand with a smile on her face. The Herbalist escorted her friend across the street to the bar and they both made their way to a pair of stools in front of the bartender. The two friends sat at the bar, enjoying the live music coming from the brass band on stage and the bartender brought them two complementary reddish orange drinks. Trinity took a sip and delight struck her tongue, bringing on a pleasant smile and Dèsirèe followed her lead. The bartender noticed they were enjoying the drinks and made his way to other customers but Dèsirèe had to find out what the drink was,

"Excuse me, but what is this?"

"Oh baby, that's my signature Voodoo Punch. Everybody come in here for it. Let me know when you want another one. But be careful, it'll sneak up on ya."

The irony of the name just made the girls fall out laughing. It was a laugh they both needed, and they welcomed the joy Mercede's Bar gave them that night. A carefree night of dancing, cheers, singing and more laughs until the sun began to creep up. That night owed them nothing and the two cherished every moment.


The next morning, a news reporter stood outside on St. Charles Avenue in front of Maison Blanche giving his viewers news of the woman that stood up against a storm. As the reporter continued with how dangerous the storm that ravage Chalmette was, Mayor Lacroix and Sonya walked out the front doors of the mansion. The Voodoo Queen waved for the reporter to meet with her on the porch and the eager newscaster rushed to her with his cameraman in tow. The reporter was so excited to have the chance to speak with the woman of the house, but he miscalled her as a mere psychic. Sonya quickly corrected him,

"Oh my dear child, I'm more than just a psychic. I'm the Voodoo Queen of New Orleans, the Oracle, the Chosen One but I will let you slide with calling me Ms. Paris."

"My apologies Ms. Paris, I'm sorry but the viewers would love to hear you tell them about what happened that night during the storm."

"To be honest I didn't come out here to talk about the storm but what came to me after the storm was gone."

"Something came out of the water?"

"It wasn't a thing that came out of the water but more of a vision. A vision of wrongdoing by a friend and a blood relative. I've been on a missing person case with Mayor Lacroix for a very long time but the names that came to me that stormy night hurt me to the core."

"Are you able to share those names with me or is this an ongoing investigation?"

"No, I came out to share with anyone that is willing to listen. The two individuals that are responsible for Chalmette's loyal Deputy Sheriff Milson are Dèsirèe Glapion and my sister Trinity Paris. They were in Chalmette that night and they assaulted Officer Milson during a regular traffic stop, then stuffed him in their trunk."

Sonya began shedding tears in front of the camera, pulling at everyone's heartstring as she gave her rendition to what happened that night. She handed the reporter a copy of what she claimed was the police dashcam of what happened to Officer Milson. Mayor Lacroix then stated there was an APB out for the two women and that if anyone saw them to call his officers. What many didn't know was that Sonya had her faithful followers in the city of Chalmette put together a made-up video. She got her shapeshifting worshiper Baka to imitate the missing officer conducting a traffic stop. The video showed two women beating and stuffing an unconscious Officer Milson in the trunk of a car, then driving away. Law Enforcement all over the city was in an outrage, looking for revenge and searching for the two women that hurt one of their own. The Voodoo Queen had set another trap and added the icing on the cake with a plead to her sister as she stared into the camera with tears in her eyes,

"Trinity please turn yourself in. I know you didn't mean it and I know it's scary, but I'll be right there with you. Do the right thing."


Trinity woke to Baaloo cussing at the television newscast of an anchorman calling for the arrest of the two women who kidnapped a Chalmette Sheriff Deputy. The Herbalist wiped the sleep from her eyes as she tried to focus on what the Voodoo Priest was talking about. Dèsirèe sat there in disbelief listening to the news report saying how dangerous her and Trinity were. It even stated how they went on the run when Sonya confronted them about the sheriff's disappearance at their workplace. Dèsirèe laughed at the report,

"Really? We ran? More like the bitch was trying to kill me in that store."

Trinity chimed in saying that it was time for them to fight back and not let her sister tarnish their names or pit the whole city against them. Baaloo was fed up with how the city of New Orleans's Voodoo Oracle had twisted the faith so much to benefit her. Even though on the video they continued to replay over and over again of a deputy being assaulted, he could see through the illusion that it was his twin. The three faithfuls were ready for battle, and no one could stop them from heading out. Trinity called on her protector **Loa Brise** and the mighty Spirit appeared, ready for war. When they walked out the front door, dark storm clouds rushed in over the city with rumbling thunder announcing something serious on the rise. The boss of the woods, **Brise,** stormed off ahead of them, in search of any adversary of the three and the trio followed behind. The two armed guards who watched over the house had no choice but to follow behind Dèsirèe and her crew. They were instructed to call Senator Patterson if anything happened, and they did just that. The Voodoo trio had jumped in a car outside of the house and sped down the street with nothing but facing Sonya head-on. Baaloo drove with aggression, weaving through traffic, but his two passengers were completely calm, pulling in all the positive energy they could find. They both meditated on what they had to do, speaking with their Spiritual counterparts. Trinity spoke with the very first *Loa* to ever approach her, *Loco,* the guardian of sanctuaries and he blessed her with strength to face her fears. Dèsirèe invoked the very powerful *Loa, Papa Legba,* who was just as ready to defeat his own brother, *Kalfu*. The car they were in turned on St. Charles Avenue, the massive oak trees that outlined the street seemed to hover over the road. The streetcar that went down the median and the elaborate mansions on the street were a constant reminder of the eloquence the city held. The antique streetlights with French-inspired names of the roads they crossed, carried merit with them all. A history that few understood but many praised was in jeopardy. Dèsirèe tried to understand how something so beautiful had such a grimy underbelly and Sonya was at the root of the problem. They were getting close to Maison Blanche and the hairs on Trinity's arm raised up but a black tinted SUV pulling in front of them stopped any advancing. Baaloo thought NOPD finally caught up to them and Sonya won but when the doors opened to the big vehicle Councilman Jackson got out,

"What are y'all doing?"

"Finishing what she started."

"Dèsirèe, you three are no match for the firepower she has at that mansion. Every guard, every maid, every butler is armed and willing to take you out in her honor. They are ready for war."

"So are we."

The Councilman heard a voice behind him and when he turned to see who it was, there stood the Chou brothers. Phuc and Tran Chou set for battle, plus they brought their entire clan of Vietnamese gang members with them. A slew of cars with Chou's gang members blocked all of St. Charles Ave, waiting for instructions. Dèsirèe cried as she walked up to Phuc Chou, hugging him, knowing why he and his brother were there,

"Phuc, I'm so sorry. I was supposed to protect her."

"No, you don't get to apologize Da Den. Bian knew what she was getting into and she wouldn't have had it any other way. Wipe dem tears. Now it's time to fight."

The entire Vietnamese BTK gang shouted in their native tongue as they left heading up the street and Dèsirèe left with them. Trinity followed behind but before she walked off, she looked at Councilman Jackson,

"I do believe we got enough now."


After her appearance on the daily news the Voodoo Queen perched herself on her throne pleased with the trap she set. She patiently waited on one of her trusted followers to bring her details on the capture of Trinity and Dèsirèe. Sonya was gloating at the fact that she felt she outsmarted her enemies, but ***Zaka*** appeared with a sinister smile on his face,

"You simple minded city folk always thinking you're better than the common man."

"What are you talking about? Everybody is out to get them. They have nowhere to run, nowhere to hide. They will be locked in chains, thrown in a cell and eventually become victim to my blade. I won."

"Haha, like I said, simple minded. Who said they are hiding? Open your eyes."

"I'm sick of your riddles. What are you talking about?"

"Open your eyes."

Sonya thought the ***Loa*** was just messing with her and ignored his statements until she heard noise outside of her office door. Baka came rushing through the office door shouting for Sonya to get to her sacred room. The sounds coming from the rest of the mansion sounded like a civil war going on. People were screaming in agony, growls and groans echoing through the halls with sounds of furniture breaking. Baka grabbed hold of Sonya's wrist and they made their way to the stairs that led up to her sacred room. A large grey wolf charged down the hall towards Sonya as she headed up the stairs. The animal was the most vicious creature to stand before her, and it was heading to her with rage in its eyes. Sonya's guards stood in front of her with automatic weapons and opened fire on the beast. At that moment the armed men found themselves face to face with the powerful *Loa Bosou,* and one swing from the iron chains in his hand took them out. Sonya ran up the stairs terrified that the powerful Spirit was right behind her, but he was busy bashing in the heads of every opponent that came his way. She locked the double doors behind her, locking Baka outside with the three-horned beast but again even Baka wasn't on *Bosou's* menu. The Voodoo Doctor scrambled past the massive Spirit as it continued its rage but found himself rushing in the arms of his twin. Baka laughed when he stood in front of the man who looked exactly like him holding a wooden bat,

"Long time brother."

"Yes, long time."

"You would be involved with this scurry of roaches invading my Queen's mansion."

"One thing you can say about roaches. A nuclear bomb can't get rid of 'em."

"But a good poison will make them all drop like a rock."

Baka then blew a white dust in his brother's face and took off running as Baaloo tried to wipe the powder from his eyes. Staring through blurred vision, Baaloo attempted to chase behind his evil twin. Shadows of bodies darted pass him as sounds of battle filled his ears. Baaloo ran behind who he believed was his brother and his sight began to clear but a haze was all over everything. He stood behind a man standing over one of Sonya's dead guards but when the man turned around, he was one of the Vietnamese gang members. Baaloo went to look in another direction for Baka but then flashes of his brother's face showed in the gang member's face. He swung the bat in his hand as hard as he could at the shapeshifter's head and Baka revealed his true identity. Baka fell to the floor as he smirked,

"You always had a sight beyond illusion."

"No, I could always see through yo bullshit."

"So, what now little brother?"

"You might be ten minutes older, but I was always the wiser one."

Baaloo snatched his brother up by the shirt, but he didn't see the blade. Baka buried the knife in Baaloo's side, and his reaction was to swing the bat at his twin's head. The Voodoo Doctor blocked the blow with his forearm, but the wooden bat shattered the bones in his arm. Baaloo collapsed to the floor and his twin Baka ran off through the crowd of people.


The disruption coming from the other side of the double doors of Sonya's sanctuary room had her cowering in the corner. She frantically prayed for her master to come save her, but the mighty *Kalfu* was nowhere to be found. Sonya could still hear the three-horned *Loa Bosou* dominating every soul that attacked him, but she could tell from the screams and destructive sounds the powerful Spirit wasn't coming up the stairs toward her. She kneeled down in front of her altars as she continued to pray for help. The room filled with a thick mist and Sonya finally received an answer to her prayers. The room glowed red, the evil laughter from a woman echoed out and iron chains dragging the floor followed with a thumping sound. The fog thickened, the sacred room glowed bright fire red, and the she-devil *Marinette* walked from behind the altar with her husband *Ti-Jean.* The red Voodoo Witch smiled at Sonya as she held out the back of her hand to be greeted,

"Kiss the ring servant, I brought you some help. Cause you look like you need it."

"Where's Kalfu, I called for him and he still not answering me."

"Kalfu comes when he wants and right now, he's not coming to help you. I suggest you take what's given to you."

A tall faceless *Loa* by the name of *Bakulu* walked from behind the altar dragging iron chains behind him. *Bakulu* stood 8ft tall, slender in stature, dressed in a black suit with a black tie and iron chains hung from his wrists dragging the floor. The faceless *Loa* looked menacing and even without a face or complete lack of any facial features, ***Bakulu*** growled like an angered beast. Sonya didn't know what to make of the Slenderman *Loa,* but she welcomed his aggressiveness as he charged the doors towards the outside noise. ***Bakulu*** tore the double doors from its hinges with one swipe of the chains attached to him. The two fierce *Loa* stared at one another with ***Bakulu*** standing at the top of the stairs and the powerful ***Bosou*** standing at the bottom of the steps. The three horned *Loa* had two henchmen palmed by the heads and tossed them off to the side when he saw the slim demon charge down the stairs. Running full speed, the two *Loa* met in the middle of the staircase and thunder erupted in the mansion. The powerful Spirits attacked one another viciously, like a battle similar to a lion and a hyena. With ***Bosou*** finally occupied with an opponent that could match his power, *Marinette* aided Sonya in her escape out the altar room. The she-devil escorted the Voodoo Queen down the hallway as the dwarf ***Loa Ti-Jean*** snatched souls up, sending them to a fiery underworld. Even though he had only one foot the fire ***Petro Loa Ti-Jean*** moved down the hall with precision, eliminating anyone in his path. Sonya could see the front exit of Maison Blanche and thought she was escaping the hostile takeover. Poison Ivy and green moss grew wild all over the walls of the mansion, as if it was chasing the fleeing Voodoo Queen down the hall. There were only a few feet between her and the outside world when a wall of vines, 10 feet tall, crashed through the floor stopping her escape. Sonya could hear her little sister's voice behind her,

"Where you going big sis?"

They all turned around to Trinity standing at the other end of the hallway, surrounded with an array of thorned vines and brightly colored flowers. The dwarf **Loa Ti-Jean** charged towards Trinity, but his advances were halted by protective vines that quickly snatched him away and buried him in nearby bushes. Sounds of him struggling to get free were muffled by the rustling leaves that took him away. Sonya couldn't believe her little sister was strong enough to make a Spirit disappear so quickly before her eyes. She knew going into battle with her sibling right now wasn't going to end in her favor and began to back down. The she-devil *Marinette* was a warrior by nature and advanced towards Trinity,

"Bitch, she may be scared of you and your vegetation but yo little leaves don't mean shit to me."

"I definitely don't want you to be scared. Scary people are dangerous."

The **Petro Loa Marinette** became even more angered at Trinity's sarcasm, summoning flames to grow from her hands. The flames burned down the hall, scorching everything as *Marinette* made her way to Trinity and the Herbalist stood her ground. Every step the angered Spirit made was a fiery footstep closer until the she-devil was in arm's reach but then the **Loa Loco** appeared in front of Trinity,

"Now now Marinette. That's enough."

The Voodoo Witch's rage became unstable, and she swung at the Spirit of Vegetation but in a flash, **Loco** subdued her in a coil of vines with the wave of his hand. As quick as the powerful Spirit came, he disappeared into the foliage covering the walls with his captured **Marinette** following behind. Sonya was all alone and for the first time terrified at what may happen. She backed up into the wall of vines and a few animated as if they were snakes, snapping at their victim. Trinity didn't see her sister as the all-powerful Voodoo Queen she portrayed herself to be all that time, she could see fear in Sonya's eyes. The entire Maison Blanche was in an uproar with gang members battling out with armed guards, Voodoo Spirits going to war with each other and Trinity witnessing Sonya's reign was almost over.

Dèsirèe was standing in the middle of the grand hall and marveled in what she was witnessing. The regime her ex-best friend put together was falling apart right in front of her. She never thought the connections she made during the time she was away would come back as her aid in helping her save the city she loved.

Dèsirèe stood untouched as havoc literally went on all around her, the Chou brothers stayed close by as protectors of her, but the Voodoo Oracle had a spiritual protection also. Powerful *Loa* like *Brise, Ayizan, Erzulie* and *Ayida* all watched over her from all four corners of the room. Dèsirèe was heavily protected as she made her way through the mansion. She noticed her three spiritual companions move about through the chaos. Lucas along with Laveau's daughters stood as reminders to what everyone was fighting for. To right the wrongs brought on through the religion Dèsirèe found herself loving so much. Her spiritual friends smiled at the woman she had become and gloried in what she accomplished. Auras of anger, love, fear, peace, greed, and much more coursed through every soul in the building. The battle between good and evil went on right before her eyes, but a bright aura suddenly appeared, making its way towards Dèsirèe, as a silhouette of a man formed. *Papa Ghede* also known as *Baron Samedi* walked up to her with a smile on his face. Barefoot wearing a black top hat, a black tailcoat, black slacks, and dark glasses, the dark Spirit tilted his hat as he greeted her. Dèsirèe was on guard against the Spirit,

"You are not wanted here devil."

"Devil? No my child. I'm not evil nor good but I'm surely no Devil. But I have been known to have some devilish ways."

"You've been in Sonya's ear this whole time. So, to me you are a devil."

"I only told her what she wants to hear. Her desires never held good intentions, so that's what I fed on. And I must say, she fed me well."

"Be gone."

"Not quite yet, you succulent jewel. I come bearing gifts. Looks like you'll be the one feeding me today."

**Baron Samedi** handed Dèsirèe a black curved dagger with a silver skull on the handle. The dark Spirit exited the same way he came, and the Voodoo prophet was left with the blade resting in her hand with no clue to what his statement meant. Dèsirèe left the grand hall and stepped in the hallway to find the standoff between the Paris sisters. She watched as Sonya begged on her knees for Trinity's forgiveness and the Herbalist released tears of sorrow for her sister. Trinity was ready to reach out her hand, forgiving everything her sister ever did to her but Dèsirèe could see the whole picture. A black tentacled Spirit slowly rose from the floor behind Trinity and before Dèsirèe could even shout to warn her, the powerful **Kalfu** emerged from the blackness. The evil Spirit snatched Trinity by the neck, slamming her against the wall and all of the greenery the Herbalist created withered away. **Kalfu** put his nose close to her face and inhaled deeply, smelling Trinity's essence as he squeezed tighter around her neck,

"No getting away from me now little flower."

The Voodoo Devil relished in finally capturing the one soul that could have beat his servant and Sonya joyed in her master's triumph. They both underestimated Dèsirèe as she called on two very powerful Spirits. The old man **Papa Legba** appeared on the side of his brother **Kalfu** and gently removed his hand from around Trinity's neck,

"Not today little brother, not today."

The evil Spirit of Death was beyond pissed that his brother came to interfere and pushed **Legba** to the floor. A bright white light flashed and bursting through the light was the very powerful **Loa Damballah.** The large serpent God grabbed hold of **Kalfu** by the head as the rest of him coiled around the mighty Spirit. Sonya could only watch as her master struggled, but his struggles were useless against the powerful **Damballah,** and **Papa Legba** calmly talked to the angered brother of his,

"Let it go brother. Light will always conquer the darkness. These children have played in your game long enough."

The lost soul in Sonya knew if **Kalfu** was done for so was she and made a final attempt at ending her sister as she charged towards Trinity with vengeance in her eyes. Dèsirèe jumped in between the two, stopping Sonya in her tracks as Trinity stood in shock. The two best friends finally stood face to face with each other and looked down at Sonya's mid-section. The blade that was given to Dèsirèe was buried deep into Sonya's belly and her life fluid started to spill over the holder's hand. The defeated Voodoo Queen fell victim to the one that was there to dethrone her, and Trinity cried out for her big sister,

"No Sonya! No!"

*Kalfu* disappeared into a black mist from *Damballah's* coils and the old man *Legba* comforted Dèsirèe with a smile as he vanished. Trinity fell to her knees and rested Sonya's head in her lap as the light in her sister's eyes began to fade away. Dèsirèe feared with her act of being a saving force she created an enemy and slowly backed away from the Paris girls. The Herbalist reached out for her friend's hand,

"It was something that needed to be done and I knew once I saw her face, I wasn't going to be able to do it. Thank you."

"Trinity, I'm sorry."

Maison Blanche fell silent; the war was finally over, and everyone began tending to the wounded. The last few breaths from Sonya became more and more shallow but the night wasn't finished. The bright aura Dèsirèe saw earlier appeared again and the infamous *Baron Samedi* stepped out, kneeling down next to the fallen Voodoo Queen. The *Loa of Death* came to collect and reached down in Sonya's chest, pulling her soul from her body,

"I'll be taking this with me. Thank you."

The powerful Spirit left with Sonya's soul in his grasp and Baaloo staggered over to his friends after getting himself up from the injuries his brother inflicted on him. Grateful for the ones that were around her, Trinity placed her hand on Baaloo's wound, a bright light emitted from her palm and the Voodoo Priest's wound was healed.

The Voodoo Doctor Baka scurried down a dark Saint Ann Street, holding his shattered forearm, looking for a place to hide himself. He laughed hysterically that he escaped the ravaged Maison Blanche with his life and everyone he shared the house with became a distant memory. Baka knew he needed a safe house to hide away in so he could recover because he knew if Baaloo wasn't dead, he would come looking for him. He slipped in and out of consciousness as the pain from his arm grew but the ill-natured soul pushed himself as he tracked down the street. Baka found himself in front of a house on St. Ann, where two innocent residents were sitting on the stoop having a beer and talking. The two men concerned that the distressed man needed help got up to assist him,

"Say man, you good?"

Whispers buzzed past the deranged Voodoo Doctor's ears like a fly at a picnic table. He swatted at nothing, and the two men became more concerned believing the visitor was having a breakdown. The whispers stopped but a devil set in the shapeshifter's mind. With evil intent in his eyes Baka sliced one of the men across the side of his face and pushed the other to the ground, stabbing him in the leg. Enraged with evil Baka went to inflict one deadly blow to one of the men when a light-toned black woman appeared. She was dressed in early 19th Century clothing, with a turban wrapped around her hair and a shawl over her shoulders as her dark burgundy dress dragged the ground. The woman opened her hand and blew a white powder in Baka's eyes. The Voodoo Doctor dropped the blade as he fell to the ground and the yellow woman disappeared into the night as a whisper could be heard,

"Enough is enough."

Baka's eyes rolled to the back of his head, he mumbled indescribable languages and the two injured men called for the police as they held the crazed man down. The two men couldn't believe they were just attacked in such a manner and talked amongst themselves,

"Man what the fuck! Came here for a vacation and I end up getting stabbed. This city is crazy."

"When they told me who this house was for, I should have known something weird was gonna happen."

"What the hell you talking bout?"

"Dawg, 1020 Saint Ann Street. This *Marie Laveau* house bruh. You didn't know? Why you think it was so damn cheap?"


## *OUTRO*


Balance came back to the city of New Orleans with the downfall of the old Voodoo Queen and with Sonya gone, her spells over all the powerful people of the city was broken. Senator Elizabeth Patterson took over as Governor of Louisiana and Councilman Trevor Jackson took the rings of being Mayor of New Orleans. All the other mayors along with police force stopped searching for the two women in the fabricated video after Officer Milson mysteriously showed up alive at a fishing dock, still wearing his uniform. The sheriff's deputy told everyone he was embarrassed about being a dirty cop and ran away to get his mind right. The incident at Maison Blanche was classified as another lavish party that got out of hand and the police are still searching for the suspects that vandalized the building. The crazed man arrested after the knife attack on St. Ann Street was transported to a psychiatric facility, but he later escaped. The only video available was of a light-toned woman walking out of the man's room dressed in a vintage 19th-century Victorian-style dress with a head wrap on her head. After a few weeks, Baaloo's Spiritual Voodoo Temple and Community Center was up and running and open to the public. He served meals to the homeless, provided a rehab center for the addicted, taught classes and gave sermons to anyone that wanted to learn the religion he so loved. Trinity stepped into the status of being named the new Voodoo Queen of New Orleans. She didn't want the responsibility because she didn't want to end up becoming like her sister, but her friends convinced her that her heart wouldn't allow her to. Dèsirèe went back to a craft she fell in love with in Vietnam. She opened a tattoo shop on the outskirts of the French Quarters. She decorated the shop with pictures and artifacts from all over the world, to remember all the people who helped her along the way. Dèsirèe became an ally to the Vietnamese community and a Spiritual Counselor to the Chou family. On occasion during her deep meditations, she would be blessed with visits from old friends she loss. Lucas and Bian, always carrying a smile for her. Order was truly back in the city of New Orleans, but it also had three individuals that watched over the Voodoo Realm to keep the peace.

# The Most Popular Voodoo Loa and Their Description

- ***Ayida:*** *The female counterpart Ayida: The female counterpart*

- ***Agau****: Agau is a very violent god. Earth tremors and the frightening sounds associated with storms are because of Agau. Agau is angry. Those who are strong enough to keep him in their bodies are puffing with all their strength and sputtering like seals. One has to be very strong to harbor this spirit.*

- ***Sogbo and Bade*** *(the loa of lighting and wind) act together and call upon Agau, a thunder storm is produced.Agau is the inseparable companion of Sogbo.Bade and Agau share the same functions, loa of the winds.*

- ***Agwe:*** *(Agive) He is invoked under the names "Shell of the Sea," "Eel," and "Tadpole of the Pond." Sovereign of the sea. One of the many lovers of Erzulie. Under his jurisdiction come not only all the flora and fauna of the sea, but all ships which sail on the sea.*

- ***Ayezan: (Aizan, Ayizan)*** *This is Legba's wife. She protects the markets, public places, doors, and barriers, and has a deep knowledge of the intricacies of the* *spirit world. Selects and instructs certain novice houngans.*

- ***Ayida:*** *The female counterpart of Dumballah, his mate, is Ayida. She is the mother figure. She is the rainbow. Together they are the unitary forces of human sexuality. Her symbol is also a serpent. She is quite submissive and very delicate. Her co-wife is Erzullie. It is said that whoever "can grasp the diadem of Ayida will be assured wealth" (Metraux, p. 105). Also known as Ayida Wedo: her job is that of holding up the earth.*

- ***Azacca or Zaka:*** *This is the loa of agriculture but is generally seen as the brother of Ghede. For this reason Ghede will often come to the ceremonies for Zaka and come when Zaka has mounted someone. Zaka is a gentle simple peasant, but greatly respected by the peasants since he is a very hard worker. He is addressed as "cousin". He is found wherever there is country.*

- ***Bade:*** *The loa of wind. He is the inseparable companion of Sogbo, God of lightning. He also shares his functions with Agau, another storm spirit.*

- ***Bakulu:*** *(Bakulu-baka) He drags chains behind him and is such a terrible spirit that no one dares to invoke him. His habitat is in the woods where offerings are taken to him. He himself possesses no one. Since no one wants to call on him,* *people simply take any offerings that go to him and leave them in the woods.*

- ***Bosou Koblamin:*** *Violent petro loa. Bosou is a violent loa capable of defeating his enemies. He is very popular during times of war. He protects his followers when they travel at night. Bosou's appearance is that of a man with three horns; each horn has a meaning–strength, wildness, and violence. Sometimes Bosou comes to the help of his followers, but he is not a very reliable loa. When a service is held, Bosou appears by breaking chains that he is restrained. Immediately upon appearing he is given a pig, his favorite food. The ceremony in honor of Bosou always pleases a congregation because it allows them to eat. Usually a good number of people attend such a service.*

- ***Brise:*** *Brise is a loa of the hills. He is boss of the woods. Brise is very fierce in appearance. He is very black and has very large proportions. Brise is actually a gentle soul and likes children. Brise lives in the chardette tree and sometimes assumes the form of an owl. Brise is a protectorate. He is strong and demanding and accepts speckled hens as sacrifices.*

- ***Congo:*** *A handsome but apathetic loa. Content with any clothing and eats mixed foods with much pimiento and is fond of mixed drinks.*

- ***Dumballah (Dumballah Wedo, Damballah):*** *Known as the serpent god, he is one of the most popular. Dumballah is the father figure. He is benevolent, innocent, a loving father. He doesn't communicate well, as though his wisdom were too aloof for us.*

- ***Erzulie: (Ezili)*** *Erzulie is the female energy of Legba. She has tremendous power and is feared as much as she is loved. Also, she has several different roles: goddess of the word, love, help, goodwill, health, beauty and fortune, as well as goddess of jealousy, vengeance, and discord. She is the ability to conceptualize, the ability to dream, the artistic ability to create. She is the female prototype of voodoo who represents the moon. She is the most beautiful and sensuous lady in the voodoo pantheon. She is respected and wealthy; wears her hair long; is very jealous and requires her lovers to dedicate a room for her ritual lovemaking. Erzulie is not a loa of elemental forces, but THE loa of ideal dreams, hopes and aspirations. As such she is the most loved loa of all. She is known as the earth mother, the goddess of love.*

- ***Erzulie Jan Petro:*** *Violent spirit loa belonging to the Petro tradition. Jan Petro is called upon to take responsibility for the temple where spells are on display; although she is a neutral entity, when not called upon it is the duty of the* *devotees to make them behave peacefully or violently, depending on their motivation for dealing with the spirits. Jan Petro as a protector of temples is very powerful; when people come to the temple they soon find out. Jan Petro likes fresh air and water; she is a sea spirit. She likes perfume and lotion–any temple dedicated to her usually smells like lotion, for it is thrown on those things she possesses.*

- ***Ghede: (Papa Ghede)** Ghede is the eternal figure in black, controlling the eternal crossroads at which everyone must someday cross over. His symbol is the cross upon a tomb. Known as the spirit of death, other spirits fear him and try to avoid him.. Ghede is also often called BARON SAMEDI. In this aspect he is DEATH. He is the keeper of the cemetery and the primary contact with the dead. Anyone who would seek contact with the dead must first contact and solicit Ghede/Baron Samedi in the same way that Legba is contacted to cross over to the spirit world. Another of Ghede's great powers is as the protector of children. Ghede generally does not like to see children die. They need a full life. Thus he is the loa to go to when seeking help for a sick child. Ghede has the power over zombies and decides whether or not people can be changed into animals. Any such black magic voodoo must seek the help of Baron Samedi/Ghede with these tasks. Lastly,* *since Ghede is the lord of death, he is also the last resort for healing since he must decide whether to accept the sick person into the dead or allow them to recover.*

- ***Gran Boa:*** *Lives in the deep forest where the vegetation is wild. He is the protector of wildlife, and doesn't like to be seen. He eats fruits and vegetables all day in the woods and when called in a ceremony, he is usually not hungry but the people always have food for him anyway. He is the loa that must be called upon before one is ordained into voodoo priesthood.*

- ***Grande Ezili:*** *An old woman, crippled with rheumatism and she is only able to walk by dragging herself along on the ground with a stick.*

- ***Jean Petro:*** *Jean Petro is a deformation of Don Pedro, the name of the Spanish slave. Jean Petro is the spirit-leader of a group of strong and violent spirits called petro. The difference between the good loa (rada) and the evil loa (petro) is still far and wide. Voodoo services are rarely held for petro loa; however, they still do occur but most services are for family and rada loa. Some say that Jean Petro was brought about by Don Pedro who was a Negro slave of Spanish origin. He acquired much influence by being denounced as the instigator of some alarming plots to overthrow the* *government. Because of this he symbolizes resistance, force, uprisings, and a sort of black power ideology.*

- ***Kalfu (Carrefour, Kalfou):*** *Legba is twined with his Petro opposite. Kalfu too controls the crossroads. Actually, were it not for him the world would be more rational, a better place. But, not unlike Pandora in Greek religion and myth, Kalfu controls the evil forces of the spirit world. He allows the crossing of bad luck, deliberate destruction, misfortune, injustice.Kalfu controls the in-between points of the crossroads, the off- center points.Legba controls the positive spirits of the day. Kalfu controls the malevolent spirits of the night.Yet Kalfu can control these evil spirits too. He is strong and tall, muscular. People do not speak in his presence.*

- ***Kongo Savanne:*** *A fierce petro loa. He is malevolent, fierce, and strong. Savanne eats people. He grinds them up as we would grind up corn. His color is white. He is a loa not to be messed with.*

- ***Krabinay:*** *Krabinay loa are petro loa. They dress all in red and do high impressive jumps. People are warned away from Krabinay. However, they are very tough and can offer a great deal of assistance to a houngan.These loa behave in a truly devilish way. Possessions induced by them are so violent that spectators are advised to* *keep their distance. They take pleasure in cynicism. However, they undertake treatment of desperate cases.Despite their admission of creation by God they avoid mentioning his name.*

- **Legba:** *Old man who guards the crossroads. He is the origin of life, so he must be saluted each time a service or any other activity with the loa will begin. Legba controls the crossing over from one world to the other. He is the contact between the worlds of spirit and of flesh. He can deliver messages of gods in human language and interpret their will. He is the god of destiny and is also the intermediary between human beings and divine gods. Legba is one of the most important loa and he is the first loa to be called in a service, so that he can open the gates to the spirit world. Allowing humans to communicate with other loa. No loa dares show itself without Legba's permission. Whoever has offended him finds himself unable to address his loa and is deprived of their protection. He is the origin and the male prototype of voodoo. Voodooists believe that if Legba grants their wishes, they can contact the forces of the universe. He is the guardian of voodoo temples, courtyards, plantations,, and crossroads. He protects the home*

- **Loco: (Loko)** *is the spirit of vegetation and guardian of sanctuaries. Mainly associated with trees. He gives healing* *properties to leaves; the god of healing and patron of the herbs doctors who always invoke him before undertaking a treatment. Offerings are placed in straw bags which are then hung in its branches. He is only recognizable by the pipe smoked by his servant and the stick which he carries in his hand. His favorite colors are red and white. Animals that are most likely to be offered to this god are black or white goats or russet-colored oxen. Portrayed in the form of a butterfly, Loco has an extensive knowledge of pharmaceutical uses of herbs. It is said that Houngans and Mambos receive their knowledge from Loco. He is known for his good judgment; often during conflicts he is called in to be judge. He is known for his intolerance of injustice. It has been said that he transforms into the wind and listens to people without them knowing he is there.*

- ***Marinette-Bwa-Chech:*** *Literally "Marinette of the dry arms." This is a petro loa or an evil spirit. Worship of her is not spread all over Haiti but is growing rapidly in southern parts. Her ceremonies are held under a tent and lit with a huge fire in which salt and petrol are thrown.She is most dreaded; a she-devil; the sworn servant of evil. She is respected by werewolves, who hold services in her honor. She is an agent of the underhand dealings of Kita who is, herself, an outstanding loa sorceress.The* *screeching owl is the emblem of Marinette.*

- ***Ogoun:*** *(Ogorin, Ogu-badagri) Ogoun is the traditional warrior figure in Dahomehan religion. He is quite similar to the spirit Zeus in Greek religion/mythology. As such Ogoun is mighty, powerful, triumphal. In more recent time Ogoun has taken on a new face which is not quite related to his African roots. This is the crafty and powerful political leader. However, this political warrior is much more of an image of where struggle is in modern Haiti.Originally, he was the god of blacksmithing; however, now that blacksmithing has become obsolete, he has become the warrior loa.He can give strength through prophecy and magic. It is Ogoun (Ogu) who is said to have planted the idea and led and given power to the slaves to the 1804 revolt and freedom.*

- ***Petro:*** *Comes from a new nation of spirits forged directly in the steel and blood of the colonial era. They reflect all the rage, violence and delirium that threw off shackles of slavery. The drums, dancing, and rhythm are offbeat sharp, and unforgiving, like the crack of a rawhide whip. The Bizango is an extreme form of the Petro and it is sometimes described as the wild Petro. Bizango occurs by night, in darkness that is the province of the devil.*

- ***Siren and Whale:*** *These two loa are marine divinities, so closely linked that they are always worshipped together and celebrated in the same songs. Some people say the Whale is the mother of the Siren, others that he is her husband; others say they are used for one and the same deity. Popular opinion says the Siren is married to Agwe. When Siren turns up in a sanctuary, the person possessed by her appears simply in the role of a young coquette most careful of her looks, and speaking in French, often offending the peasant servitors. Both the Siren and the Whale are often viewed as "upper class."*

- ***Ti-Jean-Petro:*** *This is a black magic or "petro" loa that is depicted as a dwarf with one foot. Even though Ti-Jean-Petro has a French name, his roots can be traced back to Africa. He is easily comparable to a spirit that roamed through the bush. This spirit, too, was depicted as having only one leg. This loa often protects and assists black magic sorcerers. Ti-Jean-Petro also is recognized under the names of Petro-e-rouge, Ti-Jean-pied-fin, Prince Zandor, and Ti-Jean-Zandor. He has a violent and passionate nature that becomes apparent when he mounts people.*

*Source: Author: Jan Chatland. "Descriptions of Various Loa of Voodoo"– Spring, 1990.*